A DEATH IN THE FAMILY

Steve Townsend

Best Wishes
Steve Townsend

UPFRONT PUBLISHING
LEICESTERSHIRE

ISBN 1 84426 018 6

First Published 2002 by
MINERVA PRESS

Second Edition 2002 by
UPFRONT PUBLISHING
Leicestershire

A DEATH IN THE FAMILY

For Alison, my wife and best friend.
For Ann and Roger, my parents for their support and
encouragement.

Lord Dunning was dead.

This in itself was not considered to be a bad thing by those who really knew him. The general consensus of opinion was that Lord Dunning was as popular as a dose of genital herpes. It was the manner of his death which caused the problem.

And even in death, this odious being still made his influence felt, impacting upon my life, and not in an essentially good way. But to begin at the beginning, where it all seemed to start to fall apart for me, we need to go back, way back.

My name is Cole Meredith, but first, a little about me so that you can see where I'm coming from and how I got myself involved in this, my first real case.

Let's face it, coming from a five generation family of police officers, it was an absolute certainty that once I left university, armed with my doctorate in criminology and an 'A' level in alcohol abuse, picked up after years of selfless practical experimentation, I would take up the family heirlooms, handcuffs, truncheon and notebook, but have you ever noticed how life throws you a curve when you least expect it?

It came as a devastating shock when the police forces of six counties replied: 'Oh… sorry and everything but you're just too goddamn short.'

I mean let's look at this problem in some depth. I have the brains, the brawn but not the height? I began to realise then and there why crime was on the increase and detections were down. Police officers were no doubt running around the country measuring each other. Not that I am biased or hold a grudge you understand. Needless to say, my father did his constabulary nut.

Mother was very comforting, as mothers generally tend to be, repeatedly saying, 'Good things come in little packages.' I think it was meant to encourage or at least reassure me. It didn't work!

My little sister, Maria, inherited all the positive attributes from my mother's end of the gene pool. She had gone to medical school and had just completed her finals. We confidently knew she would pass but would she get the result she craved? With three doctors in the family, two medics and me, my father seemed to become very withdrawn and spent much of his time mumbling about where he went wrong. In his eyes, I had become the failure of the family and, when mother was out of earshot, he reminded me of the fact.

He went as far as to bring home brochures about companies whose claim was 'Hite-O, the wonder drug! We can increase your height without surgery, just send £9.99 to…' He had hundreds of these, or rather, I had hundreds of these, they appeared miraculously after every visit by my parents. I once considered sending the money and trying it out, but after a few more drinks I decided 'Nah, stuff 'em.'

Even as the failure my father considered me to be, I seemed to be doing all right for myself. Lecturing at Bradley University in Shropshire was bringing in enough of the readies to keep me comfortable and, with a little nest egg put aside by Mum and Dad, I was getting by.

Though Dad considered me a disappointment, the great white hopeless, all I could say in defence was sue my DNA. Humour was lost on father, it was easier getting a drink out of him than a laugh.

And then of course, Murphy with his unavoidable laws played his hand, just for good measure; the day after I signed a five-year contract with the university, fixing my very nice salary and position within the teaching faculty, the British Home Secretary stood up in the House of Lords and announced to the world how wrong it was that the British Police Service were losing so many potential recruits from the ethnic minorities because of the height issue, and so, with immediate effect, this unfair custom was to be finished, except for the City of London.

My father arrived within the hour, application form and references already completed, just awaiting my signature. I explained at some length, some words with more than two syllables, I admit, that it was now out of the question, unless of course I wished to take a salary decrease of something along the lines of ten to fifteen thousand pounds a year; walk out of a very comfortable and, I might add, stress-free nine to four job in a nice warm lecture hall with sixteen weeks paid holiday and, forgoing all this, join a public service which worked unhealthy shifts, in all weathers with only four weeks holiday a year. I weighed up the pros and cons. As I was growing up, my father and grandfather would tell me the tale of when God made police officers which went something like, 'When the Lord was creating police officers, he was into his sixth day of overtime when an angel appeared and said: "You're putting a lot of fiddling around on this one." And the Lord said, "Have you read the spec on this order? A police officer has to be able to run five miles through alleys in the dark, scale walls, enter homes the environmental health inspector wouldn't touch and not wrinkle the uniform.

'"They have to be able to sit in an undercover car all day on observations, cover a murder scene that night, canvas the neighbourhood for witnesses and give evidence in court the next day.

'"They have to be in top physical condition at all times, running on black coffee and half-eaten meals, And they have to have six pairs of hands."

'The angel shook her head slowly and said, "Six pairs of hands… No way."

'"It's not the hands that are causing me problems," said the Lord, "It's the three pairs of eyes the officer has to have."

'"Is that on the standard model?" asked the angel.

'The Lord nodded. "One pair that see through a bulge in a pocket before they ask 'May I see what's in there, sir?' (When they already know and wished they'd taken that accounting job). Another pair here on the side of their head for their partner's safety. And another pair of eyes in front that can look reassuringly at a bleeding victim and say "You'll be all right ma'am." When they know it isn't so.

'"Lord," said the angel, touching his sleeve, "rest and work on this tomorrow."

'"I can't." said the Lord, "I already have a model that can talk a twenty stone drunk into a patrol car without incident and feed a family of five on a civil service pay cheque."

'The angel circled the model of the police officer very slowly, "Can it think?" she asked.

"'You bet," said the Lord. "It can tell you the elements of a hundred crimes, recite cautions in its sleep, detain, investigate, search and arrest a gang member on the street in less time than it takes five learned magistrates and judges to debate the legality of the stop… And still it keeps its sense of humour.

"'This officer also has phenomenal personal control. It can deal with crime scenes painted in hell, coax a confession from a child abuser, comfort a murder victim's family, and then read in the daily paper how law enforcement isn't sensitive to the rights of criminal suspects."

'Finally, the angel bent over and ran her finger across the cheek of the police officer. "There's a leak," she pronounced. "I told you that you were trying to put to much into this model."

"'That's not a leak," said the Lord, "it's a tear."

"'What's the tear for?" asked the angel.

"'It's for bottled up emotions, for fallen comrades, for commitment to that funny piece of cloth called the national flag and for justice."

"'You're a genius," said the angel.

'The Lord looked sombre. "I didn't put it there,' he said.

I realised, with this additional pressure by my father and grandfather, it made things much more difficult, and with their definition of a what a police officer should be and should do, I knew that I did not have the ability, drive or dedication to live up to their expectations and decided in less than a second, I was better off in the education field, not law enforcement, no matter what the roaring old buffoon insisted was best for me.

My social life was remarkable though, marking papers, preparing lectures, teaching Aikido at the local gym, and for my female students at the university, I was turning into a social leper, the kiss of death to any function I was invited to, I usually found myself in the kitchen towards the end of the night, probably washing up.

God only knows what my young lady, actually saw in me (she keeps telling me not to use this term of introduction about her, she insists that she is her own person, and I am nothing but a sexist pig, and admittedly, as I am a practising fully paid-up chauvinist I continue to introduce her as my young lady). Well, to be honest I do know, but that's my not so little secret.

My young lady, a quaint terminology you'll notice. Well, in this particular case, I consider it very accurate. She is young, twenty-threeish, although I would estimate she is a little older, but creative chronology has always been a female prerogative; she being a few years younger than myself, I am considered to be a lucky individual by my peers, for Judy was a lady, in every sense of the word, deed, manner and title.

Lady Judith Dunning.

A real English rose, the catch of the campus. For being a crashing bore by my colleagues' standards, I was having the last laugh. And mine, because on occasion, she said so, but it had to be the right occasion of course and generally involved copious amounts of champagne and pâté.

I remember we had been going together for a year or so, when we decided (although in hindsight I recall it was, on the whole, her idea – I think I was there just to make the numbers up), to get spliced, married, to shuffle gracefully out of bachelorhood. My track record suggested quitting while I was ahead and accepting.

'Cole,' she said one morning over breakfast, which consisted of croissant, orange juice and coffee for her, something dead swimming in cholesterol-free oil slicks for me, 'Mummy and Daddy are having a bash next weekend, do you think we could go?'

Now breakfast generally implies morning, early morning in most cases, which in turn suggests still being tired. Which of course means that most of your brain is still functioning in the twilight zone and common sense is trying, mostly in vain, to break through the pâté and champagne fortress; built the night before on the battlefield of over indulgence.

'Er… yes,' I replied.

I, like most men, know that that is usually the correct answer to a question you didn't really listen to.

I remember scratching my stubble overrun chin, whilst my lone, overworked and alcohol laden deductive brain cell, which was functioning alone and without the aid of a net and currently enthusiastically operating all my bodily functions, managed to deduce the fact that it must be a weekend, probably a Sunday due to the well known practice that, whenever possible, I resist the temptation to join civilisation and never shave during the weekend. This I feel gives me the chance to get back to my Neanderthal roots, and saves my disposable razor blades for the business week when I really need them.

Now, it must be stated here and now that Judith's parents were rich. No, perhaps that doesn't go far enough, they were not just rich, not even vaguely filthy rich but when talking about the family bank balance, you got the distinct impression that looking in the dictionary under the heading RICH would just state the family name and address.

When checking Judy's bank account, it took a while to differentiate between the balance and the telephone number of the branch. I could give examples for ages about Third World countries with a smaller bank balance but never mind, I think you can get the general idea.

Now the family weekend house was on a small island south of good old England.

I had heard Judith talk about it before, reefs, Porbeagle shark fishing from the family boat, about a mile or so out in the Gulf Stream. The little village down by the family harbour, the family church for those fear encouraged attacks of religion. You can probably tell that I am not a being who follows any religious behaviour in any guise.

Religion, I feel, is for those people who need a crutch to lean on when times are bad and then clutch desperately to it when things get better, just in case.

My view, for what it's worth, is that there is nothing wrong with other people believing in supernatural deities who control our destinies and have a contact in the galactic planning council, (after all anyone who can build a planet in six days must have a been a union man. I can't help wondering though, if this God chap does exist, and if he did or does; did he get planning permission)? It strikes me that every religion has at its core the same fundamental belief, only the names have been changed to protect the innocent, and yet people still keep fighting about who is using the right name.

If people feel that they need religion, fine, as long as they don't try to peddle it door-to-door like household cleaning products or ever so useful kitchen utensils. Then I think everyone is entitled to believe in whatever, as long as it is harmless and does not affect me, in any way, shape or form. Anyway, soap box time over, the Dunning family were impressively very wealthy, so you see what I mean about being rich?

Now islands and I get on great, as long as I get to stay in the middle and the island in question has a name like the United Kingdom, Asia or the United States.

I'm not a coward or anything like that, but the sea is big, deep and decidedly unfriendly, one-to-one I can handle, but there are seven seas and they tend to stick pretty close to one another.

You understand, don't you, it's not really the sea that scares me, it's, well, okay yes it is the sea, I just hate that much water.

Well, I had said that we could go, and before I had finished my breakfast, Judith had phoned the mainland homestead and told them to expect us.

It was about midday when I finally began to think properly and also the time Judith informed me what I had agreed to. Well, shall we just say I was deeply upset.

'That was unfair, Judy!' I scolded, wagging a finger at her.

'What was?' she asked, using the same tone she generally reserved for instances when confronted with the telephone bill and my credit card statements. Butter wouldn't melt? More like it would never get the opportunity, evaporation setting in first.

'Dropping that party on me first thing this morning, you know what I'm like during the mornings, especially during weekends!'

'You mean you don't take any notice of me?' The tone in her voice had changed and hundreds of generations of the male survival instinct kicked in. The throwaway comment was a warning shot across the bow.

Judy was adopting the traditional female attack posture, she was pouting and her clenched fists arrived strategically on her hips, I noticed her foot beginning a rhythmic tapping. Alarm bells in the back of my mind went off with clockwork-like precision.

'That's not what I said,' I began, desperately attempting to back water. My arms flew up in the gesture of surrender. I knew when I was outgunned and didn't relish the thought of facing off against this particular adversary.

'No,' she conceded, 'but it's what you meant!'

It never failed to amaze me, it was a power my mother, sister and now Judy were able to call upon with embarrassing frequency, they could interpret what I was really saying when I hadn't said anything at all, and they knew exactly what I meant when I myself was as surprised to discover what it was I had really meant as they were.

It was slightly disturbing to know that I could be misinterpreted by those around me with such ease.

It dawned on me that Judy was opting to take the easy way out of our domestic confrontation. It was another tactic employed by the other women in my life, notably my mother and sister. The method itself was easy enough. Firstly change the subject, catch the male off-guard by getting him to think about something else, probably wondering nervously about where the next verbal barrage was going to land, then divert attention and next kick into high gear and pout. The next and final stage began with the tears, followed by the artillery bombardment of kitchen utensils, unwanted gifts and a highly detailed and biologically inaccurate description of what swine men were and, to complete the attack, a comprehensive and unabridged listing of my faults and failings over the last ten years or so.

I was beginning to wonder if women went to female training centres to learn the art of avoiding confrontations with partners and offspring. If this was indeed the case, the teacher must be bloody good judging by the standards displayed by her growing number of pupils.

The conversation came to an abrupt halt when I announced that we would still be going to the party but I stressed that in the future, she should wait until around midnight, when there was a higher than average chance that I was firing on all cylinders and mentally and physically able to partake in the discussion process. Remarkably, she agreed. And then came the best part of all arguments. The kissing and making up part.

It was later that same afternoon as we lay, curled up on the old worn and threadbare blue fabric of the settee, a relic that Judy had allowed me to keep from my bachelor and student years. The settee had endured many parties and close encounters without complaint from either myself or the tight metal springs of the seat's carcass. Despite its worn state, Judy and I were in full agreement, the comfort it offered was second to none.

The large flat-screened television that dominated the corner of the room was situated perfectly to enable our uninterrupted and complete viewing pleasure and relaxation. I was dozing lightly when Judy's elbow was forced enthusiastically into my ribs, prompting an immediate return to consciousness.

'Look it's Daddy on TV!' she giggled reaching for the remote TV handset.

My eyes were half closed and attempting vainly to focus by screwing up the rest of my face, the muscles aching with the varied contortions and facial exercises I was undertaking. I became aware, subconsciously of drool escaping from the right side of my mouth, edging further down my chin to where, I did not know. I deftly wiped it clear surreptitiously as I asked, 'Why, what's he done now?'

'Nothing!' she snapped back. 'Why do you always think the worst about my father?' She tossed the remote with some force on to the settee and pushed herself back into my torso, her arms wrapped tightly across her chest.

'It saves time,' I mumbled.

Her hands, quickly retrieved the remote once more, her thumb pumped the volume control vigorously, 'Shh, I'm trying to listen.'

A heavyset reporter in a poorly fitting crumpled suit and a faded grey Trilby hat pushed himself forward through the crowd of other assembled media journalists. This man was a one-person roadblock, he was thickset and obviously determined, his route was perfectly planned as he intercepted the rotund and red-faced Lord Dunning as he came down the steps of the court.

The dishevelled reporter thrust a microphone straight into the face of Lord Dunning who, in surprise, stopped dead in his tracks.

'Tim Wolfe, Scoop International Media Group!' shouted the reporter above the hubbub of the other journalists trying to be heard in vain. 'Lord Dunning, what do you have to say about the judge's decision to drop all the sexual harassment charges against you?'

Sexual harassment, I thought. Why Lord Dunning, you little devil.

Lord Dunning tried to sidestep the reporter who, despite his disproportionate build, was surprisingly more agile and quicker than the obese Lord Dunning, and was obviously used to dealing with reluctant interviewees.

'Do you have any comment about the reports of paternity testing?'

Dunning's evasions immediately ceased, I thought, well done! The reporter Wolfe had gone straight for the throat and had a result. Lord Dunning almost screamed at the reporter, the veins in his neck pumping visibly and the old man's face usually red, was starting to turn a vivid purple, I felt glad that I had paid the extra and got a colour licence to see this.

'There are no paternity tests, there never have been and there never will be! I am a good father and a happily married family man, I know and support all my children, there is no dispute and, as I'm sure that you are aware, the complainant, Miss Frobisher, has withdrawn her complaint in this matter, and I will not be seeking any legal action against her, I want this to be over with now and forever. Any further comment will be made through my lawyer, Stephen Carpenter. Now good day!' And with that, the juggernaut of a man who was Lord Martin Dunning, was pushing his way past the reporter.

'Yes but…'

'I said no comments, speak to Carpenter if you want any further statements!' The camera pulled back and tightly focused on the smiling round face of the crumpled journalist.

'And there you have it, the blackmail case which has been heard in court two today has been convened, the complainant, a Miss Frobisher, a personal assistant to Lord Dunning during his time in a government post has been dropped with no evidence offered by the complainant. Lord Dunning has declined to make any counterclaim against this woman, and is now happy to get back to his private life. Neither Lady Dunning nor Miss Frobisher were available for comment today. However, the legal costs against Miss Frobisher are believed to be several tens of thousands of pounds; which this reporter has learnt has been paid already by an unknown benefactor. I'm Tim Wolfe, Scoop International Media Group.'

I turned to Judy, 'All his children? I thought you were an only child?' I reached past her and pressed the off button on the remote, the TV blinked into darkness, the screen crackling with released static electricity.

'I am, that is obviously what he meant, he's just playing it safe, that reporter was twisting his words, you know what they're like.'

I knew that, although there was plenty of mileage in discussing the topic further, it was not worth the aggravation. I simply asked, whispering quietly, 'Did you know about this court case?'

She shook her head, pulled away from me and picked up her books. Silence reigned. I knew it would only be over when Judith broke it.

Later, as we both sat in the lounge, without looking up from the reference books and copious notes she was studying, Judy broke the lengthy silence asking, 'Will you please try and get on with Daddy this time?'

The question caught me a little flat footed. After all, as far as I was concerned, we had sorted out the dispute about the family party earlier, by now it was early evening, and I was putting the finishing touches to Monday's revised lecture on serial killers in modern society, once again.

'Sorry?' I put the pen down and removed my reading glasses.

Judy put down her folder, I noticed that a Mills & Boon novel was also within easy reach of her and couldn't help but wonder which of the two texts held her attention the most.

'I said will you make an effort to get on with Daddy this time?'

The question took a few seconds to sink in, it always seemed that wherever Judy's father was concerned he could do no wrong, it was always left to me to make the effort, I regularly doubted the effort was worthwhile.

'Yes,' I sighed in genuine resignation, I knew that the situation between father and daughter would never change.

'I'll make an effort if he will,' I added, under my breath for obvious reasons.

'It will be a good opportunity for you to unwind.' She stated matter-of-factly, 'I mean you don't even have to take your mobile phone.'

'Oh, and why not?' I asked. Judy knew that I never went anywhere without my trusty mobile.

'Well, it's up to you, but Daddy won't let them put up any of those transmitter things on the island and, the geology, something about the type of rocks on the island, means they wouldn't work anyway.'

'A natural black spot, without the aid of a tunnel?' I queried.

'Yes, if you like, there are phones on the island of course, Daddy isn't a complete technophobe, he just thinks that mobile telephones are a curse and he bought the island years ago when he discovered that they won't work there.'

'Great, so I get a weekend with your father without the opportunity of a fortuitous phone call summoning me back to work for an emergency exam sitting,' I stated, returning my attention to the papers, the tone in my voice enough to tell Judy I had reluctantly accepted my pending fate.

'Good.' The Mills & Boon was picked up and Judy was away once more in the world of romance and schmaltz.

I eyed the folder she had previously been reading, the title 'A Behavioural Study Of The Under Fives In Education' held my attention for a nanosecond. Judy was a kindergarten teacher by way of earning a crust, not that she needed to work, she just liked to.

Much to her father's disgust, she simply loved children and everything they did and said. I was constantly getting reports about who did what to whom during the day, what so-and-so said to some other child, how cute they all looked for the school photograph etc. Me, well I was of the opinion that all children should be taken away for career training at birth and returned to their parents once all the bed wetting and dirty nappy stages had long past, maybe returning at the age of oh, shall we say sixteen, when they could go out and earn their board and lodgings.

I am, I suppose a hypocrite, I dislike children but get very angry when misfits of society beat or do other things to children. I secretly give heavily to children's charities but as this would spoil my image I never admit to it, so this is our little secret, although I still think King Herod had a point. Anyway, I digress, nothing more was said about the party.

The week slipped past at its usually lethargic pace, lectures, training the university Aikido team in the evenings and marking papers occupied most of my time. It was on the Thursday morning that a notable event occurred. One of my students, Eric Batheroy, had been experiencing some difficulty with some of the papers I had set and that was causing me some concern. I had spent several lunchtimes with him, attempting to get to the bottom of his recent performance slump, to no avail until today. His secret was out. Eric was going deaf and there was nothing we could do about it. Obviously he was deeply concerned about this fact and this was having a severe impact on his grades. The counsellor spoke to him today and arranged for him to undergo sign language training.

As I was leaving the campus that day, Eric was waiting for me by my car. He thanked me for my help and asked if I would be his study partner. Eric was a good student. I could only imagine what turmoil he was going through. I agreed and arranged to attend my first sign language lesson with him the following Monday. All I had to do was tell Judy that, of the two weekday nights together, one had just been cancelled, I was sure she would understand.

It just goes to show what I know about women and Judy in particular.

Friday evening inevitably arrived. I arrived home after a very heated day academia wise, it was the first night in that particular week that Judy and I had seen each other for more than a few passing moments.

The rain was falling outside, testimony to my mood, the British summertime weather had struck again, the traditional rain slamming down on to the roads, the storm drains erupting water like so many cheap imported fountains, my old car would have made more progress only if sails were an optional extra, as it was it took several students from the rugby team and a lot of shouting to get the old Rover moving off the car park so I could make this ill-fated journey home. I made my way into the flat, not so much looking like a drowned rat but bearing a more striking resemblance to the bag used to drown the rat in.

The first thing I noticed in the hallway, just inside the door was my suitcase, all packed and ready to go. Again the cerebral alarm bells started ringing in the back of my mind and I knew, without a shadow of a doubt, that the merest hint of backing out of my 'duty' at this point would be tantamount to suicide. I decided perhaps ignorance was a better tack.

'Cole, is that you?' Judith's voice wafted out from behind the closed door of the bedroom.

'Er... yes,' I replied, suddenly remembering the inevitable and inescapable party, a silent curse rising in the back of my throat and escaping my mouth in a restrained and barely audible mumble.

'I've packed everything you'll need for the weekend,' she reassured me from behind the thick closed door.

I removed my coat and hung it damp and listless on the stand next to the front door. Like a scared rabbit caught in the headlights of an on-coming car, I could not take my eyes off the cases and what they represented; boredom, tedium and potential parents-in-law. God help me.

'Oh, good... Right... Thanks,' was all I could think to say.

I made my way over to the drinks cabinet, withdrew a large bottle of Jack Daniels and poured off a healthy measure.

'Cole, you need a very stiff drink, hello.' I introduced myself to the glass of amber liquid and threw it desperately into my mouth, swallowing greedily. The warmth of the liquor invigorated me as it went about its task of removing Judy's parents from my thoughts.

Sad I know, but I find it very distasteful to drink alone, therefore on occasions such as this, I make the introductions so that I am not drinking with a stranger, well it works for me.

'Cole,' came the disembodied voice once more. 'Now listen, you've got half an hour before Daddy's company driver picks us up.'

I looked back to the bottle, considering whether there was room for one more inside, but Judy interrupted my thoughts again. 'Are you all right, Cole?' The bottle was replaced, on the cabinet shelf, the collateral damage had been done, with only one bottle of JD in the apartment, I knew there was no way to dislodge the outlaws from my mind. I decided that on my Christmas list this year there was going to be an underlined and highlighted request for a crate or two of JD's best, but until then...

'Yes, I'm fine,' I sighed, taking the empty glass over to the kitchen area which adjoined the living room, very open plan.

'Are you sure? You don't sound very happy.' Judy emerged from the bedroom her slender, perfectly proportioned sylph-like body clad in blue jeans and a rather fetching red jumper.

I forced a smile, 'Yes, I'm fine,' I repeated. 'Just looking forward to meeting the mad mogul once again.'

Judy smiled a broad, warm smile which seemed to light up the room. 'Never mind, you can relax this weekend,' she said, caressing my damp brow, her mouth lightly brushing my ear, involuntarily I trembled at her touch.

'Now, jump in the shower and I'll lay your clothes out ready on the bed.'

'What, you not coming in with me?' I asked jokingly.

'No, not this time.' She gave me a playful slap and left me to it.

The chauffeur was, as expected, as punctual as ever, arriving right on time. He loaded our cases into the large boot of the sleek, jet-black limousine.

It was obvious that he and Judy were old friends. He kept referring to her as his little girl and recalling instances when she sat on his knee in the good old days.

They laughed together for many long minutes, the time seeming to pass slowly as I looked on, a stranger to these joyous, playful memories.

Judy giggling like a giddy schoolgirl as she recounted the many times she had helped him wash the cars and the inevitable water fights that ensued.

I tried to get into the conversation several times to a short, curt, 'Yes sir, very good, sir, excuse me, sir,' from the chauffeur without him even breaking the sardonic grimace he seemed to keep reserved just for me.

Judy appeared not to notice my discomfort. I could see this weekend was going to be a bundle of fun. And so, just to keep the excitement at the same raucous fever pitch of excitement and merriment, I had secretly packed a pile of my class's midterm papers, essays and theses, just for good measure.

See, I said the weekend was going to be exciting.

The trip down south took far longer than I had anticipated. Commuters, roadworks and the general volume of traffic added to my travelling misery.

The snail-paced holiday traffic, the weekend caravans and the persistent weather serving to keep our speed down to a crawl. I noted several times we were passed on the pavement beside us, by the same geriatric anarchist with a zimmer frame, his one-fingered salute to us in the limo as he passed us and we passed him just about summed up my feelings about the whole damn journey.

As a result of the poor travelling time, Judy slept most of the way while I tried to make the most of a bad lot, and marvelled at the scenic views I caught glimpses of in the street lighting, as we progressed into the onrushing darkness and rain. I felt glad I was actually inside and in relevant comfort, even though the chauffeur, Jefferson, with the communication and conversational ability of a brick, ignored my attempts at striking up a conversation, leaving me to talk at him for the last hour of the journey.

By the time we had reached the small fishing harbour of Marlbury Port on the south coast, the rain had stopped once again. Now it was the turn of the wind to make its presence felt.

As we drove along the old narrow stone quayside, I could see the wind was whipping up the waves, picking them up and smashing the watery destruction down on to the quay with wild abandon. Just looking at this was making my knees feel decidedly jelly-like.

Jefferson dutifully unloaded our cases, or to be more precise, Judy's several large, heavy cases and my overnight sports bag and briefcase. As this mammoth task ensued in the howling wind, I made my way timidly to the edge of the quay and looked down into the raging torrent at the small matchstick-like vessel moored securely to the iron bollards set firmly and securely on the quayside. The vessel appeared small, only about forty-five feet in length from front to back, or whatever the damn nautical terms are. With a virgin clean and immaculate white paint job it looked helpless against the combined onslaught of wind and sea.

A depressingly young and athletically built man emerged from the cabin on the floating coffin, and, waving to us enthusiastically, leapt nimbly on to the steps of the quayside which led from the craft to us. The man's natural timing, jumping from the boat on the rising crest of the wave, revealed his familiarity with all things nautical. I knew instinctively two things: firstly he had done this many times before, and secondly, his dashing, rugged good looks, athletic physique and energetic welcome for Judy made me dislike him instantly.

'Good evening, sir.' He stood in front of me, all teeth and tan, six feet tall and nearly as broad, deep electric blue eyes, piercing in their intensity, peered out cheekily from beneath his shoulder-length sun-bleached blond hair, his muscular physique straining beneath the confines of his clothes and taut skin. Muscles seemed to race and ripple along his arms, each trying to make way for another muscle, which was desperately expressing a keen interest in making its presence felt, he seemed oblivious to the cutting wind and ice from the sea spray.

He extended his right hand enthusiastically towards me in a gesture of welcome and I grasped it automatically. And so began the age-old custom of the battle of the vice-like grip. After a few seconds though, it appeared I was the only one playing. The man viciously pumped my arm with youthful, playful vigour, he appeared genuinely pleased to see us.

I could see maintaining my dislike for him was going to take some work.

'We're ready to go whenever you are.' The man spoke with a deep Cornish accent, one of those which made you want to reply 'Ooh arr!' and leap into a conversation about cream teas and local pirates of note.

The man was about eighteen or so, a good six inches taller than myself. He was wearing a tee-shirt and shorts. In this weather, to my eyes, he looked ridiculous, but he never seemed to acknowledge the forces of nature, merely flicking the wind-blown debris from his hair and face only when he could no longer see.

'Mark!'

The shout issued from behind me on the quayside from the direction of the now empty car.

Judy came running along the quay to join us. With arms outstretched, she clasped him to her.

'How are you and the family? Are the boats in good shape? There's so much I want to ask you, how have Mom and Dad been?'

She pushed herself away, holding him at arms length and stared lovingly at him, scanning him up and down, taking in every rippling muscle and toned lump. I decided at that point, disliking him just got a hell of a lot easier. Almost reluctantly Judy turned away from the gigolo, she called to me, 'Cole, this is…'

'Mark. I know.' I interrupted her introduction. 'Can we get on to the ship please. I trust it is going to be warmer in there.'

'Boat,' corrected the tanned and smiling Mark. 'The *Try Again* is a boat.'

'Strange name,' I commented pushing past him.

'Not really, it was what my father kept telling me when I was learning to navigate these waters, every time I floundered on the rocks of the harbour, or hit the jetty, he would just say, "Try again." It's my motto, I try to live every day by it.'

I was not filled with confidence on hearing this, but decided not to show fear in the face of my adversary.

With the wind and sea in my face and hair, I jumped down the quayside steps, two at a time, the rough stone harbour steps were heavily covered with seaweed, kelp and other odd-looking sea plant life, the whole slippery and coated with a gelatinous slime.

I reached the bottom of the steps and leapt across on to the heaving, bucking, rising and falling deck. The leap must have looked spectacular, I did my best to disguise the fact that friction and I had parted company about halfway down the slime encrusted steps, and only inertia and gravity had got me on to the boat without a trip into the dark and wet harbour proper.

A jovial Cornish voice called out to me as I floundered across the constantly shifting deck, 'Takes some getting used to, huh?' Two huge, rough hands grabbed me and pulled me unceremoniously up on to my wobbling sea legs.

'It moved,' I stated in defence. I brushed myself down and turned to face the individual who had helped me back to my feet. It was my nemesis, Mark.

'Thanks,' I choked unhappily.

Judy had made her way tentatively down the kelp encrusted causeway and was standing, waiting patiently for someone to help her aboard.

The rising and falling of the deck, the constant rocking was already taking its hold upon me, the effect being simply that I could feel the vile sickly green glow rapidly spreading around my body.

I reached the right, or starboard side of the boat, just in time to display my university canteen lunch to all.

The gallant 'Sir Mark the Tanned' had done the chivalry bit and helped Judy on board. Over the noise of the crashing waves and high pitched squeal of the wind, he obviously heard my pleas to any merciful deities to either calm down the wild rolling sea, or just kill me.

'Weak stomach?' observed Mark, leading Judy across the bucking deck to the cabin.

'What do you mean weak! Look how far I threw it.' I'd been waiting to use that line for years. Now seemed appropriate, but sadly now it didn't seem that funny.

'Yes, and into wind too,' replied Mark.

He grabbed a towel from inside the cabin door. 'Here, you may want to try and get some of that stuff out of your hair and off your jacket.'

As I mopped down the regurgitated snack foods of university life, Mark smiled adding, 'Carrots again huh?'

It was definitely getting easier to dislike him, the wind was blowing puke in my face. The sea was doing its damnedest to sink us and God only knows what was waiting for me to fall overboard during a throwing fit.

Once the luggage was transferred from the quayside to the boat and safely stowed by Jefferson and Mark, the boat left the relative safety and shelter of the little walled harbour and my stomach felt like a main competitor in the Olympic gymnastic team. With the last double pike into a cartwheel and double back flip, I had the distinct feeling that my dinner stood a good chance of winning.

'Looks like a wild storm brewing,' called Mark, navigating the little craft out into the open raging sea.

'No, just sea sick,' I replied between retches.

'Sorry? Oh I see, yes very good. Now I think you had better get yourself undercover, we'll be at the island in about twenty minutes.'

'Thanks, but if it's all the same to you, I'll just...' Pause for the obligatory pasty and chip, hurl, 'Oh God, I'll stay here.'

'Whatever you say,' smiled Mark.

We'd been out only about five minutes, but to my aching intestines it seemed to be considerably longer, when the sky was sliced in two by the most brilliantly and blindingly white and silver stroke of lightning. I had been granted an eleventh hour reprieve and my guts had run out of goods to redistribute.

In the revealing flash of light I just caught sight of a small police motor launch heading back towards the mainland, it was about fifty yards or so away from us and I was only able to view it briefly as it quickly vanished from view behind a mountainous rolling wave. I realised that it seemed to be coming from the direction in which we were headed. It was at this point that the heavens again decided to open once more. I was happy being wet, it cooled me down. I was not however, happy at being here, thrown around on the open sea, like so much flotsam and jetsam.

'Trouble?' I managed to moan, making my way on increasingly shaky legs across the boat, to where Mark was lost in concentration navigating the boat through the rolling waves.

'Where?' His piercing eyes instantly scanning the waters around us.

'I've just seen a police motor launch.' He appeared to relax and return to his boat steering tasks.

'Oh, nothing to worry about, it's probably just coming back from the island, we have no police station there, usually no need,' he replied.

'Tax evasion?' I asked, brightening suddenly at the increasingly entertaining prospect of seeing Lord Dunning being dragged off in shackles to the poky. My dad would just love to see that. Hell if the truth be known, so would I.

'Good heavens, no!' Mark really sounded genuinely shocked at the suggestion.

The nausea immediately returned. And I again felt the dreadful unwanted surge in the pit of my stomach.

'Probably been there to see about the burglary.'

'Burglary?' I repeated, once more thoughts of a professional interest in this weekend away perking me up, the sick feeling fading away. Perhaps this would be an interesting break after all. 'Tell me more about it if you can, it'll take my mind off the Technicolor yodel.'

'Nothing to tell really.' He shrugged, his huge sinewy arms wrestling with the wheel as he spun it this way and that, throwing the small boat through low breaks in the constantly shifting waves, aiming for the smooth part of the waves as they rolled passed us. 'Someone broke into the house last Wednesday night,' Mark continued, his concentration fixed as he tried desperately to navigate the small boat through the swells.

'Get away with much?' I asked. I found myself wondering why on earth, in this day and age did we continue to use this primitive mode of transport to get around. I was then painfully aware of something warm and decidedly unfriendly rising in the back of my throat.

I found it hard to believe that I had anything else left to regurgitate, but my stomach had found an otherwise unknown and untapped store and dragged it out with a vengeance, shuffling the mysterious find and preparing to hurl it northwards.

'Not really, just a few guns and some bullets, I think they said one of them was a rifle,' shrugged Mark.

'That all?' I was a little shocked at the tone and the dismissive attitude of the little sailor boy. Over a number of years, I have become very familiar with many types of firearms, both theory and practical applications. Machine guns and rifles I have a particular dislike for. The amount of damage they can cause and the range they can do it over, is frightening. But, my professional curiosity was aroused.

'How did they do it?'

'No idea, you'll have to ask Lord Dunning about that,' and that was all he would say about the matter for the duration of the rest of the journey.

Travel to the island progressed rather slowly and, other than my raw yet vocal retching talents and curses, the journey passed off quietly and without further incident. By the time we finally reached the sheltered harbour of Dunning Isle, I was wet, empty and probably smelt very bad too, however, I was thankfully spared this aromatic torture as my nose was completely clogged with sea salt and worse things.

Mark piloted the small boat into the mooring with practised ease and expertise. From my kneeling, prayer position at the side of the boat, I could see several burly middle-aged men moving quickly across the rough stone quayside as Mark slowed the boat, and then casually threw thick ropes up to the men who caught the wet heavy ropes with ease and looped them over the strong metal anchor points on the quayside which stood like iron sentinels in defiance of the relentless elements.

Back on terra firma, I felt human once more, my colour and ability to stand upright returned.

I felt and if I do say so myself, looked, considerably better than I had done since getting on the boat and undertaking this violent sea crossing. The ravages of the wind and wild sea could not penetrate the harbour with its full effect, despite its constant attempts to violate the thick stone walls of the harbour, something to do with the design of the harbour and its clever positioning on the island, I was later informed.

From down here at the moorings on the quayside, I could see the fairy lights of the Dunning presidential palace burning and twinkling away on the crest of the steeply rising wooded hill, some distance above the small fishing village.

Somewhere in the far distance, a church bell mournfully tolled the half hour.

Behind me, the wind, rain and rhythm of the crashing waves against the harbour walls induced a dreamy, relaxing euphoria that swept me up.

'Ready to face the family?' It was Judy, at my side and smiling sweetly. She held a huge golfing umbrella high over our heads, shielding us both from the harshness of the English summer weather. She screwed up her tiny yet pert button nose and laughed, saying, 'You smell sickly.'

'Gee, thanks,' I replied in mock distaste, 'and yes, I'm ready to face the wrath of the Dunning empire.'

A small horse drawn buggy was waiting for us at the end of the jetty. And it was with some relief that we clambered aboard and closed the doors behind us, shutting out the terrible weather and trapping in the aroma of my mal de mer. Like a fairy tale, the buggy clattered off, across the cobbled stone roadways and out on to the hardened dirt tracks of the island, along tree-lined avenues and then round and up into the steeply rising hills, copses and lightly forested bluff of the isle, following the single uneven and worn dirt track as it snaked up into the night, high into the heart of the Dunning's island.

As the church bell struck nine in the near distance, I felt the buggy shudder to a halt, the noise and feel of loose gravel under the carriage wheels and the hooves of the horses arousing my curiosity. I looked out of the cab through the narrow closed unshuttered window of the buggy, to see that we had pulled up in a large gravel strewn circular in and out driveway, several tens of yards across.

The house itself was all lit up, blue white carbon lighting highlighting and exaggerating the beautifully crafted stone work of the place. Built in the same style and design as the White House in Washington DC, I couldn't help feeling that it seemed completely out of place, here in England. Although the pretentiousness of Lord Dunning helped to remind me that he probably did consider himself to be the president.

The house was large, domed and only slightly smaller than the original. I half expected to see a slightly smaller stovepipe hat wearing bearded president, burst through the double oak doors at the top of the front steps, shouting a hearty address to his fellow Americans.

The house was colonial in style, large stone columns and windows all around it, the carbon lighting giving it a cold blue white look against the patchy, cloudy, starry night, the thick rolling clouds high above had given us once more a temporary reprieve, and called a cease to the relentless downpour to which we had been subjected to for most of the day and night so far.

I noted that two sets of stone steps rose sweepingly out of the gravel driveway, in perfect symmetry they arced away from each other, turning back and eventually meeting ten feet higher at a wide balcony, which I later discovered ran around the entire periphery of the residence.

Judy and I clambered down from the romantic horse-drawn buggy, the driver already away on his chore of unloading the luggage, the stench of my clothing accentuated by the enclosed buggy cab.

I made to go towards him and help, but Judy's restraining hand on my arm stopped me.

'Leave him to it, it's his job, you're a guest here.'

I was about to protest when she simply clutched my hand and squeezed it reassuringly.

Nothing more was said between us, nor was it needed.

Hand in hand, for both mutual security and confidence, in unison, we simultaneously took a deep breath and climbed the steps to the wide front door. The colonial design of the house was similar to that I had seen in the old American civil war movies.

To me, it seemed perfectly in character for the front door to be opened by an African American butler saying something like, 'Good evening, massah,' that too would seem to be in keeping with Lord Dunning's well documented, voiced and popularly resented bigoted views, but no. The door was opened by a young looking man, in his mid- to late twenties, probably about my own age, but looking considerably younger. He was only a few inches taller than myself, he stood upright and stiff, the epitome of what an English butler should look like. His light brown hair was neatly groomed, gelled back almost flush with his scalp with an air of permanency that would defy anything to cause a hair to move. He was clean shaven and his features remarkable only in the fact that they were unremarkable, his nutty, hazel eyes revealed nothing about the man's demeanour, other than what he allowed the outside world to observe.

He was wearing the traditional, and I would hasten to add, ridiculous looking long black tail coat, black bow tie and waistcoat over a pristine white shirt, his shoes clearly patent and expensive in appearance. I got the impression that he was due back in the wedding outfitters window soon.

'Miss Judy, how wonderful to see you.' The man's clipped and polished voice revealed no trace of an accent. He looked down his nose and acknowledged me with a barely noticeable nod. 'Sir.'

'Donald, how lovely to see you too. How's Mary?' Judy, was barely able to hide her excitement as another old friend was added to her rapidly growing list. The penguin disguised as Donald the butler led us into the hall.

I was impressed I have to admit.

The floor was pure white marble, ornate statues and bronze busts lined the heavy oak panelled walls, old masters, probably original works adorned the walls. A wide marble staircase rose up through four floors towards the stained glass domed roof above us.

Suits of armour, highly polished and ready for the next battle with an array of pointy weapons to choose from, stood guard here and there and the heads of executed wildlife hung from any conceivable support. An abattoir would have had less death in it.

The only source of light came from high above us, a huge crystal chandelier, supported by thick chains hung down from the stained glass dome.

'Mary is very well, thank you. We are married now you know,' continued Donald.

'Oh, I'm so pleased. Congratulations to you both!'

'Thank you.'

Arm in arm, Judy and I followed the butler into the waiting room just off the main hallway, the door to which was cleverly disguised as part of the oak panelled wall. I wondered how many other rooms were disguised in such a way, and how many I had already walked past without realising. And then, once in the waiting room, I knew I had entered the lair of the dreaded parents.

The room was again gothic in decoration, thick dark carpets

on the floor, flickering gas wall lights and a roaring open log fire in a stone grate, a red leather reading chair and large sofa arranged neatly before the fire, dominating this room.

The walls were lined with bookcases groaning under the strain of thousands of old leather covered books.

The only distasteful thing to my eyes in this room, other than Lord Dunning himself, were the many and varied animal skin rugs which I noted with growing anger were real.

Lord and Lady Dunning turned to face us as Donald opened the door and led us into their gothic lair.

'Mummy, Daddy!' Judy ran across the room, arms spread wide.

Lady Dunning received the greeting like all mothers, openly pleased to see her daughter home safely, but also determined not to spill anything from the nearly full whisky tumbler she clutched so desperately.

Living with Lord Dunning, I could easily understand why she felt the need to crawl into the bottom of a bottle now and again.

Lord Dunning was standing facing the roaring, crackling fire, his back towards us. He was wearing a scarlet paisley smoking jacket and looked like a pimple about to burst. I had the feeling either fashion wasn't his strong point, or he had a previously unheard of sense of humour. I decided that his obvious lack of fashion sense was the only correct choice, and not for the first time.

He glanced quickly over his shoulder and turned away in disgust when he noted that I too was present.

'I see the parasite is still with you,' stated the smoking jacket slowly turning fully around to face us. He was as rotund as I remembered from my previous meetings, the television failing to give scale to his true bulk. I noted that since our last meeting, his eating utensils had not been idle, with perhaps a couple of extra new chins he had been working on since puberty, were now well established and were coming on nicely.

I realised that his attitude towards me had not diminished either.

'Still teaching?' His tone told me this interest in my career was not out of parental interest or concern for his daughter, it was a comment designed simply to ensure I knew my place, and to remind Judy where I fitted in the great scheme of the rat race.

'Lecturing,' I corrected. 'Yes. And you sir, still fiddling investors and screwing the hired help?'

'Cole. How good to see you.' Lady Dunning jumped verbally into the fray, distracting both the bloated old man and myself from further barbed exchanges. Just in time too, I noted, judging by the colour Lord Dunning's bulbous head was turning, his face and jacket now matching perfectly.

Lady Dunning interjected at precisely the right time, not bad for someone half-cut.

'Judy told me you would be coming so I've put you in the west wing. Mark has had your luggage brought up and Donald is unpacking it now.'

'My daughter will of course be in her own room, not in the west wing,' added Lord Dunning.

'I can assure you there is no need for that, I do not mind sharing with Judy,' I replied, forcing a smile and looking directly at Lord Dunning.

'In my house, I assure you there is every need for it and you will sleep where I damn well tell you, under my roof...' I had heard the 'under my roof' speech many times before at my parents' house, usually when I had tried, in vain, to entertain young ladies there.

'Yes, Daddy, that will be fine,' interrupted Judy giving me the 'shut up or lose me forever look'.

'Thank you,' was all I could think of to say.

Shrugging the situation off, I sat heavily on the old cracked leather sofa.

'Have you eaten yet?' asked Lady Dunning.

Despite her poor taste in men, I found that I actually liked her, she was always interested in the welfare of others, even if her husband would never let her act upon her interests.

'No, not yet Mummy,' replied Judy, looking at me with a knowing twinkle in her beautiful blue eyes.

'Cole?'

'No, I haven't eaten thanks. I really don't think I can face food at the moment. The sea was a little unkind.' I gestured to my drying puke encrusted slowly stiffening clothing.

'Oh, I see.' Smiling, she excused herself saying she was going to arrange Judy's meal. Leaving, for the time being, Judy and myself alone with the scarlet beach ball.

'When are you going to dump this waster?' asked Dunning, turning his back on me once more.

Not for the first time, I wished I had a knife, the perfect spot, right between his shoulder blades, an area which was visibly straining at the fabric of the tasteless paisley patterned smoking jacket just a few feet away.

'Daddy, you know Cole and I are to be married next year.'

I thought Daddy had better watch out. Judy was using her defiant voice and the 'I shall not be moved' stance, a deadly and well practised combination of female stubbornness.

'Over my dead body!' Dunning the bloated jacket spun around, his eyes flashing and narrowing, his thick blubbery lips drawn back tightly across his browning teeth, small flecks of spittle exploded from his snarling mouth in unabated objection.

'Fine by me,' I mumbled, just loud enough to be heard. I grinned and lounged back further, casually on the leather sofa, 'Shall we bring it forward six months or so?'

The idea of Lord Dunning in a coffin, doing the deep six, I felt was quite invigorating.

Lady Dunning's voice floated in from the doorway behind us, 'Dinner will be brought up in about ten minutes.'

Lord Dunning was angry, I could tell that I had hit a raw nerve, if only I could remember how, I could look forward to doing it again tomorrow. He sneered at me with a look full of hate and his huge frame barged past me, storming out of the room, slamming the door with such force that I felt sure that the door frame would be smashed off.

'You don't need to rush, I'm sure there will be enough food, even for you!' I called after him. Judy stared at me, her expression one of disdain. I almost felt guilty, but the feeling soon passed.

From behind the heavy door, I could hear the unmistakable tones of Lord and Lady Dunning exchanging angry words at about two hundred decibels.

'I'll talk to you later about that!' Lord Dunning was shouting, the door and even the walls reverberating with the volume of his voice. Lady Dunning on the other hand was saying he was being unreasonable, which I could easily believe.

The earlier experience of the boat trip was now playing on my digestive system, which was now groaning audibly. I had heartburn in the worst way and so resolved to tackle it by drowning it with milk which I have heard can work.

'Judy, can you call down to the kitchen and order me about a gallon of milk,' I asked sitting further back in the red leather sofa, nearest the open fire, and pulling my legs up to enable me to stretch out full length in comfort. Judy crossed the room and picked up the receiver from the small occasional table by the window, she put the receiver to her ear, listened for a few seconds and then pressed the cradle several times, but to no avail, the line was dead. Obviously Lord Dunning had pissed Telecom off as well.

I decided to try the brave soldier approach and force myself through the pain barrier and to do without my bedtime milk. I was tired. After all, it had been a long day. What with university, the traffic home, the boat, the seasickness, the confrontation with Judy's father and now, all I wanted to do was sleep. This, as it turned out, was going to be easier than I had thought.

My room in the west wing was, unfortunately one floor up, half a dozen labyrinthine corridors and a guard post away from Judy's.

Her room being strategically located right next to her parents. It seems to be a universal parental obsession and obligation that, regardless of the mature age of their offspring, parents think they have a God given right to govern their children's premarital sex life.

It appeared to me, that all parents were a pain, a cross to be borne by children across the globe. Parents seemed to forget that one day their children would choose their retirement home, revenge after all, is a dish best served cold.

Reluctantly, after kissing my goodnights to Judy for too brief a time, I went to bed, alone.

It was a little after midnight when I awoke. My hormones were telling me in no uncertain terms that Judy really needed me and I should go to her without delay.

In the world outside, the wind and rain of the earlier evening had died away and peace reigned. I pulled my dressing gown tightly close around my otherwise toned naked body and quietly left the warmth of my bedroom. With practised guile and subterfuge, knowledge and skills acquired during my student days in the strict halls of residence at university, I was able to sneak cautiously across the corridor, and down the cold marble stairs.

I really wished that I, or more correctly, Judy, had packed a pair of slippers.

It was with a great deal of self-control and established sense of purpose that I was able to stifle a squeal as my bare feet made contact with the solid, icy, marble steps. On tiptoe, I persevered, at last reaching Judy's floor and the thick-carpeted hallway.

With only the parents' bedroom to be negotiated, Judy and I would be reunited, one in the eye for Daddy Dunning.

I put my ear to their door, just to ensure there was no movement and no possibility of a chance detection or potential interruption, on the other side, I heard voices.

'Martin, you're still being unreasonable,' Lady Dunning was saying.

'I've said no and I mean it. For God's sake Helen, think of the scandal.'

'Scandal! You talk to me about scandal! Look, Martin you've had the solicitor's letter…'

'I don't care, I'm warning you, I'll ruin him if you continue with this train of thought, I will not discuss this any further, the answer is and always will be no, now get that into your stupid drunken head, goodnight.'

'But…'

'No buts! I mean what I say. Forget it or I'll ruin both of you! You know I'll do it.'

So, as mother-in-law to be was obviously standing up for Judy and myself, I decided that perhaps on this occasion, discretion was the better part of lust and reluctantly resolved to leave Judy alone in her room. Holding back my frustration, I crept back to the ice cold biting marble stairway.

Noting with painful realisation that each step was considerably colder than its immediate predecessor, I was encouraged to climb the stairs faster and faster, taking the steps two or three at a time, reducing my points of contact as much as possible.

Reaching my own warm and comfortable bedroom once more, I dived on to the bed, pulled the bedclothes over my head and went straight to sleep, sleeping soundly until the early morning when I was rudely and viciously awoken.

I was torn from the comfortable, protective arms of Morpheus by an exceedingly enthusiastically deployed gong being thrashed mercilessly just outside my bedroom door.

I peered through what I envisaged being tired and bloodshot eyes, through a soft diffused haze. I summoned up the strength and co-ordination to raise my left arm, moving my attached wristwatch back and forth until my eyes were finally able to decode the blurred image I was receiving. The hands on my genuine Mickey Mouse watch pointed out it was 6.30. Due to the accompanying noise of birds singing incessantly and chattering cheerily in the trees just outside my bedroom window, and the harsh, brilliant sunlight that was shining in through the shuttered window of the room, I deduced, eventually that it must be morning.

'What the bloody hell...?' I crawled out of my warm but otherwise disappointingly empty pit, ready to release my growing anger on the poor bastard who had so unceremoniously forced me from my slumber.

I stumbled blindly across the bedroom, stubbing my toe on the bedpost at the foot of my bed. This, needless to say, did not enhance my mood.

I snatched the door open and screamed, 'What the hell is going on! Is there a fire?' I know now, stupid question, but my brain was building up to the important questions like 'When's breakfast?' and 'What time does the bar open?'.

'Lord Dunning's request, sir.' Donald, the penguin, still wearing the full tails and looking like one half of the top of a wedding cake, stood with regimental stiffness in the hall outside the now open door. The gong still quaking in his left hand, he appeared not to notice my nakedness.

At this moment in time, apart from selective blindness, I failed to see if Donald had any other redeeming features. He seemed to have the same role in life as every other person on the island, in the first instance, to screw my weekend up and my life after that.

I knew that if he repeated the mistake he had just made once more during the weekend, he and I would be having words round the back of the garden shed, and only one of us would be walking back.

'Why?' I heard myself asking, my voice forcing itself through a rough, and hoarse throat, 'Why so early?'

I wanted a drink, tea, coffee preferably, but I would settle for a JD at a push.

'Lord Dunning is having a clay pigeon shoot this morning, he would like you to attend.'

'Thanks.'

The thought of me being near Lord Dunning while we both totted loaded shotguns was slightly unnerving. He was a big target and I wondered if any court in the land would believe I had shot him accidentally. It was a nice but fleeting thought interrupted by Donald who added, 'The shooting party will be awaiting your arrival after breakfast in the main hall.'

I looked at my watch again. 'And what time is breakfast being served this morning?' I asked, putting on a clipped English accent, which appeared to go totally unheeded by Donald.

'For you sir, it is being served right now.'

The breakfast was, it has to be said, excellent, the housekeeper really knew how to do a proper fry-up, something Judy had denied me since we started living together. I could understand how Lord Dunning got to be the excessive size he was. Other than being a naturally lazy glutton, I found the breakfasts alone were enough to keep a normal man going all day.

The dining room was elegantly decorated, much the same as the rest of the house. Oak panels lined the walls, the large rectangular dining table with a single heavy leather-clad seat at either end and ten symmetrically placed similar chairs along each side, dominated the room.

Dominating one wall was a long, wide cluttered sideboard, on which were a dozen bright silver covered platters, each containing rich, aromatic food. The aroma of this was noticeable from the first floor landing, wafting tantalisingly through the house. By the time you reached the dining room door, you were salivating so hard you could easily eat your own leg. The bright, clean silver cutlery, hot coffee, hot tea and ice cold fruit juices were placed alongside.

The tasteful old masters were hung here too and the whole watched over by more of the polished armour.

I would have preferred breakfast in the kitchen where it was probably a little warmer and there would be people there with whom I could at least attempt a conversation with. I felt very out of place, something I had mentioned to Judy when we last visited the Dunning homestead on the mainland.

I preferred being among the normal people, the commoners as Lord Dunning had referred to them.

I had mentioned it to him once before, that was before I knew him better as a bigoted snob. However, in the words of Lord Dunning: 'It just isn't done, but then someone of your lowly upbringing and poor station in life would of course not know such a thing.'

With the mammoth challenge of the great three course breakfast successfully negotiated and happily under my belt, and the promise of the same again tomorrow, I reluctantly left the dining hall, to find Lord Dunning, the man who had engineered this start to my day.

I remembered that I had promised Judy that I would try and get along with this tyrannical oppressive father of hers. He seemed to be at least trying to make an effort, what with the invite to join him for the shoot. It was a start, I suppose, and the very least I could do was to cooperate and endeavour not to take the opportunity to shoot him, should it arise.

Finding Lord Dunning was easy; all I had to do was follow the sound of his bellowing. I found him back in the study. He was standing, quietly now, his back to the door staring intently at the large bookcase that occupied the whole of the wall in front of him.

It was still early, and I noticed that he held a glass in one hand, a manuscript in the other; the glass was only half full, the residue of the amber liquid within revealing that Dunning had been working hard to drain the contents.

As I entered the room, I caught a brief glimpse of the title, emblazoned in two-inch high letters across the cover of the manuscript, almost impossible to miss, the title read DUNNING INDUSTRIES YORKSHIRE PROJECT.

'Done any shooting before?' he asked, not even turning as I walked into the room.

The manuscript which he had been clasping behind his back and therefore facing me, disappeared from view as he pulled it back around and in front of himself, as if it was an embarrassment or a solemn secret to which I was not privy to. The glass vanished from view too, he took two great greedy gulps from it, and when it appeared a few seconds later, it was drained.

'A little,' I replied.

He laughed and added, 'I mean real shooting, shotguns, clay pigeons, real men's sport, not the fairground variety.'

'Yes,' I replied, 'as I said, I've done some shooting, I've killed the odd clay pigeon and done some rough shooting, it's not something I'm proud of I must say, clay pigeons don't shoot back, so I don't really think it can properly be referred to as sport.'

'Right.'

He turned briskly and strode past me purposefully. He made his way to the other side of the room to a large, ornate dark wood desk. He produced a small silver key from the breast pocket of his jacket, inserted it into a lock, which at first glance easily passed for a knot in the woodwork and a part of the ornate carved scrollwork that adorned the edge of the desk. He pressed another knot mark on the desk and a drawer slid into view.

The drawer was pulled fully open and Dunning casually tossed the secret manuscript into the dark recess. Once inside, Dunning slammed the drawer shut with an audible click. The key was turned once more and withdrawn.

'What have you got in there?' I asked jokingly. 'The crown jewels?'

'Nothing for you.'

The tweed jacket he was wearing gave Dunning the illusion of extra weight, not that he really needed any more, he now resembled an over stuffed sofa with slightly fewer legs. Too many society dinners and no exercise had waged war on his waistline. It was not a war worth winning in my opinion, but obviously no prisoners had been taken and no resistance fighters remained, the home team had been thoroughly defeated.

His middle-aged spread had started early and showed no signs of either stopping or slowing down. Subconsciously I wondered if he could make a little extra cash by renting his arse out for advertising space. I considered possibly suggesting the idea to him later.

'Welcome to my armoury.' Dunning smiled and swept his podgy hands in the general direction of the bookcase.

Lord Dunning's smile was very unnerving; it reminded me of a very hungry crocodile that I had once seen at the reptile house in London, as a teenager on a school trip.

Its smile was exactly the same, just before it devoured half a cow and I could not fight the very worrying feeling that was creeping over me. The hairs on the back of my neck were standing up and I felt a shiver sprint up and down my spine.

'Have you eaten?' I asked warily, watching the grimacing face and ready to make a run for safety if it was needed.

'What?' The smile disappeared. 'Take a look.' He challenged and turned back towards the drinks cabinet near the window, through which sunlight filtered gently, braving an audience with the man.

My attention returned to the bookcase, focusing on the challenge laid down. To my eyes, the bookcase was exquisitely carved, nicely made, well built and appeared to have been designed especially to fit into its surrounds. It was cluttered with old, dusty leather bound books, mostly classics, but apart from that, it was totally uninteresting.

Nothing noteworthy.

Dunning hung his head, shaking it in open disappointment. 'Useless, absolutely useless!' Dunning completed his appraisal with repeated tutt tutting, I was angry with myself, without actually knowing why or how, my prospective father-in-law had got one over on me, but it was making him happy, which was enough to annoy the hell out of me.

'And you call yourself a detective?' It was a mocking question, a scoff at my expense.

'No,' I corrected, trying to keep my temper under control, 'a lecturer in criminology and criminal psychology, actually.'

'Well, stick to that, because as a detective, you are as I expected, completely hopeless. If you take the time and look properly and carefully, you will see that this is actually the entrance to my arms locker.'

He sneered at my failure. 'It cost me an absolute fortune mind, the authorities were very impressed with it and even allowed me to keep some weapons here that I should not have, if you grease the right palms, you can get anything you want. The British police, the best law enforcement money can buy.'

I took this as a personal affront, my father was one of the hardest working police officers I knew, he was honest and always gave the other fellow an even break. To insinuate my father and his colleagues were dishonest were, to my mind, just too much.

Dunning must have seen the anger flashing in my eyes, or the vein in my neck starting to throb, for he quickly changed tack.

'Struck a nerve have I? I'm sorry about that,' he lied, 'I suppose it's almost like saying every politician is corrupt.' I knew the barbed reply was aimed at my loudly voiced opinion of him and his cohorts.

He started to pour himself another healthy measure of, from where I stood, what smelt like whisky. The crystal tumbler was nearly full when I replied.

'Yes, I suppose you're right, there must be one or two who do an honest days work!' I was angry and he knew it. He seemed pleased he had got this planned response from me, I suppose it made him feel good that he could still infuriate with the right words, knowing which buttons to press to get people to react on instinct, always a tactic guaranteed to put the defender at a disadvantage.

I realised then he was measuring my reaction, to see how far I would go in defence of my father's good name. I decided not to bite at the verbal attack and to try and change the course this conversation was heading in.

'And this is where your firearm was stolen from is it?' The retaliation had the desired effect.

'What!' he slammed the glass tumbler on to the table, sending an amber cloud of liquid splashing across the tabletop. The smug look on his face had vanished without trace in an instant. The bottle he clutched in his other plump hand almost fell from his grasp and the tumbler wobbled more and spilt the remainder of its contents on to the thick plush carpet.

His eyes were burning with fury as he spun back around to face me. Whether it was my comment or the fact that he had spilt some of his finest whisky, it was hard to say. If I had to put money on it though, I would have to say the spilt whisky was just ahead.

'Who the hell told you that?' he snarled. It was a command, not a question really, and one I felt compelled to answer, in my own time of course. It felt good to watch him squirm in his own emotions, but I could not understand why he had reacted so violently.

'Well…' I started, slowly, planning on drawing out my answer, capitalising on the enjoyment.

'Tell me now!'

I could see no real problem in telling him, after all I was under no obligation not to reveal my sources, and besides, I had no loyalty to, 'Mark, your boatman…'

'I'll have his bloody hide.' He interrupted, 'I won't have informers on my bloody payroll. I'll have him and his family out of the village and off my island by noon!'

Now a pang of conscience struck me. I had no idea that Dunning would overreact like that, I felt I had to do or say something in Mark's defence, I knew I could not let someone's, anyone's, livelihood be ruined over my petty jealousy.

'No harm done,' I quickly interjected. 'I saw the police motor launch coming back from the island and asked him about it, that's all.'

'He had no bloody right to be bandying my business around to all and sundry. What goes on here is my own affair and not to be discussed by the likes of oiks like him and you.' There was real venom in his voice as he spat the words violently at me.

'Who else knows about this arms locker?' I asked, trying to steer him away from his verbal assault and potentially not so empty threats.

He had wound up very quickly and I hoped that by changing the subject, giving him another topic to concentrate on, his pea sized whisky befuddled brain would be unable to plan and rejoice in the downfall of his boatman and his family. Besides, if Judy found out I had any part in getting the tanned one thrown out of his home, I would be in more trouble than I could possibly handle.

'What?' The look on his face was one of pure confusion as he was suddenly asked to think rather that just do. 'Oh, no one really,' he said, visibly and audibly calming down.

'Well, who exactly?' I prompted, sitting on the arm of the large red leather sofa.

'Well, obviously, Lady Dunning, Donald and his wife, the builders who put it in and the local constabulary, who come over from the mainland and routinely inspect it every month.' Lord Dunning was looking into space and counting the names off on his imaginary list, using his podgy sausage-like fingers as a cellulite tally chart.

'Donald? The Butler?' I queried.

'Yes, why do you ask?'

'Oh, no reason, just my criminologist's mind ticking over the possibilities and deducing possible suspects. Who else?' I could see the headlines now, THE BUTLER DID IT. All hail Agatha Christie.

I knew that that particular solution had died out in the movies and books of the thirties, and yet I couldn't help but wonder and start considering that particular line of thought. I have always instilled in my students not to get sidetracked like this, now in a practical situation, for the first time in many years, I was on the verge of breaking all my own rules.

'No one, that's it.'

'Are you sure? No one else at all?'

'Yes, that's it, just Helen, Donald and Mary.'

I found this all very interesting, but forced myself to think practically, this was supposed to be a break, a holiday when Judy and I could get to spend some quality time together. Away from the hustle and bustle of the academic world, the world of long hours of study, late night paper marking and lecture preparations, and here I was, asking questions about a burglary, with this man, whom I found difficult to be in the same room with.

I came round to thinking that it was perhaps better if I did not get any further involved, besides, the local police had an excellent reputation, I was sure that the investigating officers had already come to the same conclusion as I had, right or wrong. They had far more resources to utilise and other lines of enquiry to pursue, what with the builders and the employees there.

Anyway, where Lord Dunning was concerned, I found it difficult to care.

'Look, are we going shooting or what? I have been dragged out of bed to be here. If we are going, any chance we can go now so that we hopefully get to see what we're shooting at?' I decided, what the hell, I may as well get the most out of this holiday. Even if it killed me being with the evil Lord.

'Why, of course.' He beamed again; this was even more unsettling than his smile.

He crossed the room, swaying profoundly as his mass gained momentum, it was like watching some perpetual motion toy, the constant moving of his great waistline almost hypnotic whilst still being unappealing. He reached the bookcase and reached up to a leather-bound, dusty volume entitled *Great Shoots of Britain*. But instead of pulling the book towards him, as I had expected him to do, he simply pushed it back about three inches into the body of the bookcase itself.

Somewhere off in the distance there was a discernible click. Whisper quiet motors wound into life and almost silently, like some great ethereal entity, the bookcase floated backwards into the wall, pivoting on well maintained hydraulic rams back and left to reveal a well illuminated doorway and passage beyond it, that stretched away to a stone stairwell some ten feet away, disappearing downwards into the earth.

'The walls of this secret little room of mine are built on to the old wine cellar,' stated Dunning, as if this fact alone was meant to impress. 'I have, of course, had them strengthened with an additional two feet of reinforced concrete with anti drill material impregnated into the concrete itself.'

I got the distinct impression that he was reciting someone's sales blurb, probably the construction company salesman had told him that this was exactly what he needed and the price was ever so reasonable really.

'Of course,' was all I replied.

Lord Dunning led the way forward and, tentatively, I was compelled to follow.

'Well, what do you think of all this?' he asked, fishing for compliments. He was obviously very proud of this feat of engineering skill.

'Very impressive.' I was impressed; it was really an engineering marvel.

Like everything else about Lord Dunning, I found that being impressed by him was extremely irritating, but, as my dad keeps telling me, credit where it's due, besides, Lord Dunning had nothing to do with this creation except to provide the cash.

Dunning, the tour guide, led on.

Down the rough-hewn stone steps. 'Kept them for character,' he said as we walked carefully down them.

At the base of the stairs, we entered a small landing area, at the end of which was a large, solid-looking steel door with a twenty-digit numeric keypad on the left hand lintel and a six-colour panel on the right.

'Pretty complex,' I said, acknowledging the lengths to which he had gone to secure the arsenal of weapons that I was sure lay just beyond the steel door.

'Even more so than you think,' he replied, looking at his watch.

'What do you mean?'

'When we hit the first step on the stairs, we triggered a timer, we have just twenty seconds to enter the eight digit numeric code and four colour sequence.' The old man turned and looked at me. He was relishing this, I could tell.

Time was ticking away and he was explaining the system to me, but so far he had not told me what happened if you failed to do it or worse still, got it wrong.

'What happens if you don't know the code or are slow thumping it in?' I was aware of my voice skipping though the scales as I fought to keep a tether on my fear.

'Well, first of all the door to the library closes, locks and seals, then we get gassed.'

'Gassed!'

'Harmless incapacitant I assure you, and the police are notified by an independently operated radio alarm. We get an armed response helicopter from the mainland here within the hour, last time it only took them forty-five minutes to get here.'

'You do know the code, don't you?' I asked, visions of the steel door closing and locking me in here with Dunning to get gassed together, running through my minds eye.

'Don't you?' he smirked.

'Tell me you remember the code!'

'Yes, of course I do.'

He turned so his body completely shielded the pads from my view, this was relatively easy for him. I could hear his fingers rapidly dancing across the buttons as they bleeped in response until, finally, after what seemed like an eternity:

CLICK.

'Great.' The feeling of relaxation and tremendous relief swept over me like a wave.

The door swung slowly open, inwardly and another chamber came into view. The lights in this chamber coming on as the door opened, like a giant inverted fridge.

As Lord Dunning led the way onwards, into the room, I checked the heavy steel door, ten inches thick, again on hydraulic rams. I assumed some salesman somewhere was on a hell of a bonus. It was obvious that the door had not been forced; there were no marks, scratches or other signs of tampering.

'Who else knows the combination and the fail safes for the weapons locker?' I asked, following Dunning into the room.

'Only Helen and I know the combination. Helen, Mary and Donald of course know about the security devices.'

The room was quite large, it, like the rest of the corridors, walls and ceilings of the rest of the chamber, were made of the same reinforced concrete.

The room was about thirty feet long and the same wide, about fifteen high, the only light coming from several banks of fluorescent tube strip lights slung high overhead, there was a small ventilation duct high on the wall opposite where we had entered, it was about four inches square, sealed from within the room with no screw holes or other visible means of security.

The walls of the chamber were lined with racks, extending from floor to ceiling with an equally high rack creating a vast central island in the centre of the room. These racks each contained a vast array and assortment of weapons, several of which were very obviously illegal being automatics and assault weapons.

'You do have a license for all these don't you?' I asked, looking at what I knew, from several action films as being a Uzi 9mm machine gun.

'Of course.' His poker face was on, I couldn't tell if he was lying or not, but then he was a politician and couldn't lie straight in bed, I therefore concluded that the only licence he had was for his TV, and that was probably a fake.

He stood in the middle of the aisle, turned and folded his arms, with some difficulty across his vast chest. 'Well, what do you think now?'

'Incredible,' I whispered, staring awkwardly at the numerous assorted weapons of mass destruction lying all about me.

'You name it, I have it,' he said proudly and threw the challenge at me with such confidence, I decided not to take him up on it.

'What weapon was taken during the burglary?' I asked, making my way around the room, eyeing the various weapons cautiously.

'More than one actually.' He shrugged, 'Probably being used in crime even as we speak.'

'You must be very proud,' I scoffed; my eyes scanning the secure vault in shocked awe. 'What exactly were taken?'

'An M-21 rifle and a magazine of armour piercing rounds,' he replied, grabbing a pair of matching shotguns from a rack near the door.

'M-21?' I queried. 'What's that?'

'It's a sniper rifle, the American SWAT teams use them all the time,' he stated, handing me one of the shotguns and then tossing me a bandoleer of shotgun shells from a tray beside the empty racks, where the shotguns had previously rested.

I looked at the weapon he had given me, well maintained, in pristine condition, the name Purdey engraved on the plate near the butt, over and under barrels, well balanced.

'Get many uses for a sniper's rifle?' I asked.

'You'd be surprised.'

'What else?'

'An automatic pistol, 9mm Browning HP-35.'

'Any ammo?'

'Yes, just a couple of magazines, oh yes, and a noise suppresser.'

'Noise suppresser?'

'Yes, a silencer, can't have the locals complaining about small arms fire up here can we now, although I've never used it. I read somewhere that you don't actually need a suppresser, you can just reduce the charge within the bullet itself, you lose some power and restrict the range but you almost eliminate any noise too.'

'Just what you need for a weekend away from it all,' I sighed.

'Well, I enjoy my guns, I can make my own bullets if I need to, I just never get the time these days.'

He looked genuinely disappointed by this and then suddenly, his demeanour brightened.

'Come on, let's go kill some clays.' He beamed.

Closing the door behind us, we left the weapons locker.

'Where do you buy all your weapons from?' I asked suspiciously, wondering if these items had come from the black market and, more importantly, if he would admit to the fact, I didn't think he would, but it was worth a try.

'Various places really, there is a hell of a market, the rifle was from an army friend of my wife's,' he stated, 'ex-military issue. I got it for a song, along with all the accessories.' He made it sound like formal evening wear, tie clip, cufflinks, sniper scope?

'Ever used it?'

'No, damn thing has never been used. Not by me anyway, the scopes and sightings are actually very complicated things to set and use, so I have never bothered with it. He sent it over here in a large protected case about a month ago, been down here since then, until that damn thief got in here.'

We continued outside, thoughts racing through my head.

The wind had picked up once more, heralding a new storm front moving towards the island as we made our way to the cliff side overlooking the vast empty rage of the English Channel. The biting wind chilled us both to the bone as Lord Dunning and I spent a morning of destructive vigour sending the black and orange clay disks spinning and crashing to annihilation as one after the other they were launched into the air for us to destroy.

I did pretty well as it happens, but not well enough to warrant any praise from the Lord who was successful with every shot. To me it was an obvious display of a misspent and violent youth. The morning passed in relative civilness, no harsh words were exchanged between Dunning and myself, the presence of lethal firearms may have had something to do with that though.

Throughout the morning, the only words to be heard from Dunning were the repetitive single word 'pull', the order given for the clay disks to be launched before our prepared weapons.

Between us though, not a word was spoken.

It came as no surprise to me that after a very nice light lunch, Lord Dunning did not return to the shoot, a word in way of excuse came from Donald.

'He's bored and gone to be somewhere more interesting,' he informed me as he took the shotgun from me. 'We'll put these away now shall we?' he continued, unloading the weapon with professional deftness and pushing the unused cartridges back into the loose leather loops of the bandoleer.

'Well, I'm bored too, but at least I had the decency to come back,' I retorted.

'Yes, I'm sorry, Lord Dunning has quite a bit on his mind at the moment, he's not usually so rude.'

'Really?' I asked failing to understand how someone like Dunning could generate any loyalty from his staff.

'Yes, I understand that he thinks very little of you, but to everyone else, he's usually a perfect gent.'

Well, at least Donald was being honest. I wasn't sure where I stood in Donald's perception of the whole incident, and to be perfectly honest, I wasn't particularly concerned. What mattered to me was Judy's happiness and she obviously got on well with Donald and his wife, so that was pretty much it for me.

'Have you seen Judy this morning?' I asked, attempting to draw the conversation on to a topic we could both participate in.

'Yes sir, she went out first thing this morning with Mark, she should be back later for dinner.'

'Fine, thanks for that,' I felt a little flush of envy race through my veins for a brief second, unwarranted thoughts running through my mind about what Mark and Judy were up to, but then reason kicked in. I trusted Judy, she had never done anything to make me doubt her commitment to our relationship, I had no cause to mistrust her now. I made my excuses and left.

Being an adventurous sort of guy on the whole, I decided I should make the most of my time alone and pulling my thick, dark fleece coat tight about me, went off exploring the island.

The island itself was quite small, I could easily walk around the whole island in a couple of hours. But it was big enough for Lord Dunning's family to live far enough away from the small fishing village by the harbour I had seen on our arrival, to be quite isolated. I knew from our arrival the previous evening that the only harbour and village on the island lay to the north. I decided to see what mysteries lay undiscovered to the south.

It was about an hour later as I strolled along the picturesque headland; the wind blowing in from the sea was noticeably less forceful here and I had taken the opportunity to remove my coat and was now enjoying the warm summer sun when I discovered a small cove.

A rough and poorly maintained path led down through the harsh but beautiful purple and yellow gorse, down the gently sloping cliff side, to the rocks of an obviously disused wood and stone jetty, which led a short distance out over a muddy shale and rock covered beach, into the gently rolling sea spray. I had intersected the unevenly worn path at about the midpoint of its descent down the gentle slope of the rocks and gorse.

A little way in the distance to the east, about a half-mile away,

I could clearly see the spire of Dunning's private church and chapel on the other side of a dense copse of trees. Having nothing else to do and being naturally inquisitive, I made my way down the path towards the jetty, clambering awkwardly down the path side on to the slope to give myself more purchase on the uneven path.

Progress was slow, the rain from the previous days' continual downpour and the biting, spiteful and forceful winds off the sea, had, over many years, eroded much of the path, making it slippery and the rocks loose. Several times I nearly lost my footing and I consciously became task orientated, my attention focused on completing my own self-generated challenge. To reach the jetty without falling end over apex in the process, was a matter of pride.

The tide was out by the time I reached the old wooden platform, I saw that worn and tired sea eroded stone plinths supported the jetty and guided it faithfully out into the sea. I placed my thick warm fleece on the driest piece of ground I could find near the edge of the jetty where it seemed to grow out of the cliffside rocks.

The old wooden platform was evidently far older than I had first imagined and the wood creaked and groaned ominously as I tentatively edged my way out on to its uneven and rickety surface. I was about ten feet out on to the broken wooden spars when one of the mooring posts, about twenty feet further on, caught my eye. My curiosity was piqued and I felt unnaturally compelled to take a closer look at it.

It took several more cautious minutes of edging slowly forward, testing the strength of each of the wooden spars before putting my full weight on it before I actually reached the object of my exploration.

The other iron mooring posts were all barnacled and lichen covered, rusty and eroded with age and lack of use.

This one was different.

Strangely an even, worn patch several inches deep all around the base of the post was clearly visible, the barnacles, lichen and rust had been rubbed away, as if something had been moored here very recently.

I looked out over the worn and broken edge of the old jetty.

Caught in the uneven, rough surface of the wood and steel bands all along the jetty, near the worn mooring post, I saw several slivers of white paint. These flakes of paint were caught, trapped like bits of meat in a poorly maintained denture set. The teeth of the jetty had obviously bitten into the hull of some small vessel that had been moored here. Standing, I scanned the deck of the jetty, my eyes seeking out any other anomalies.

I found something quite quickly: a black gaping hole in the spars of the jetty, by the edge nearest to where the wood and steel met the cliff side, hidden partly in shadow. It looked odd and out of place.

The break was fresh; mould and lichen had not yet managed to take hold on the broken edges of the hole. My cynical and calculating mind began to grind slowly into deductive reasoning. I crossed to the hole hidden in the shadows and cautiously peered into its dark, secretive interior. From here I could see nothing but shale, shingle, seaweed and slimy unpleasant crustaceans better found in vinegar.

The old jetty was voicing its complaints at my presence with renewed vigour. The creaking and groaning of the old wood and steel jetty encouraged me to take my leave, quickly, this ancient and forgotten helping hand of bygone times which reached out into the rolling waves, was telling me either to lose weight or get off the jetty before I went through it.

With this in mind, I prepared to leave.

Carefully I edged my way across the rotten and eroded wooden deck to a partially broken and seaweed encrusted wood and metal ladder. This led down the twenty feet or so to the muddy and shingle encrusted slimy beach from which these stone plinths, which supported the broken jetty, proudly stood.

I had carefully negotiated several iron rungs that were permanently set into the wooden frame of the ladder, when, out of the corner of my eye, I spotted something caught in the lattice work of broken rotting wood and rusty eroded ironwork beneath the jetty decking.

I swung myself round and under the jetty, still some ten feet from the beach floor, and made my way through the construction, weaving my way in under the jetty. Several times I found myself having to disentangle seaweed, kelp and worse from my hands, arms, legs and face, one handed whilst I desperately struggled to maintain my grip on the filth encrusted parts of twisted jagged wood and metal beams. I kept telling myself, *there is nothing to worry about, absolutely nothing, it is perfectly safe.*

I hoped I would believe it soon and until I did, I maintained that I would not be touching these 'worse' things caught in the rafters near my head and face.

I progressed slowly, negotiating slime and broken wooden spars. Braving a fall into a muddy and tetanus demise, not to mention Judy's wrath if she saw the state of my clothing from such a fall. At last I triumphed, finally reaching my goal with no injuries and little in the way of damage to my wardrobe, to find, my goal was nothing more than a shoe.

I cursed and swore openly, long and loud. I wished I were on solid ground so that I could give myself a really good kicking.

I felt I deserved it.

A size six, black patent leather shoe – the manufacturers mark, inside the footwear was now faded and worn to little more than scratches, a 'U' and possibly an 'L' or an 'I' remained partially visible, testimony to the logo which may previously have added unwarranted bonuses to the price of this pair.

The single, solitary shoe, a little the worse for wear, was now home to a number of crabs and whelks. This crustacean shoe house retained some of its previous splendour, but I couldn't help thinking I had risked my life for bugger all. I casually tossed the offending item back into the dark recesses of the beach beneath the pier.

I felt like a proverbial prat.

I weaved my way back through the maze of wood and iron latticework and reached the relative safety of the ladder and, once back on the deck of the broken rotting jetty, I carefully crossed the rickety, whining wooden planks. Carefully I collected my fleece, determined not to get too much crap and sea debris on the fine material and then I was back on the rough-hewn path, heading east towards the chapel.

Beyond the chapel lay a broad, flat, nicely landscaped and tree-lined garden that opened eventually on the rear of the Dunning house. Somewhat dejectedly, I trudged, hands in pocket, head down, back to the house. I made a point of keeping to the path for the remainder of my trek.

The nicely manicured and well maintained lawns, mowed in even green stripes, were complete with croquet hoops, but the recent downpour of the previous evening had completely flooded it out. The hoops were half submerged. I half expected to see the metal crescents sink gracefully below the water.

Towards the house itself, the drainage problem was better resolved, although water still lay collecting unevenly in pools across the expanse of the lawn, in the main the garden resembled a well kept mire. The once fine and picturesque landscaped garden now looked well at home as an advert for trench warfare.

I negotiated the narrow stairway up to the low balustraded balcony that circumvented the house. I looked in the patio windows of the dining room at the rear of the house and checked my own appearance as my reflection was cast back at me. Yes, I looked a bloody mess, slime and crap all over me and now encrusted and caked into the fibres of the fleece coat, Judy's present to me just two weeks previous.

But the only thought in my head that was really of any great consequence at the moment was that I really and desperately needed a shower.

'Good heavens, Mr Meredith,' Donald gasped as I made a fairly dramatic entrance into the kitchen.

'It's my impression of Lord Dunning's personality and hospitality,' I replied light-heartedly. Mary who chose this point to re-enter the kitchen released a strangled scream as her eyes met the abomination that had just entered her haven of peace, harmony, hygiene and tranquillity.

'Sorry, I didn't mean to scare you,' I said, attempting to redress the balance somewhat.

'My kitchen!' she screamed. 'Get out! Get out! Get out!' Like all the women in my life to date, Mary was completely unwilling to listen and let me explain.

She failed to understand my dilemma or take into consideration how I felt about the situation. She just ejected me back out into the garden. At least Donald was understanding and went some way to be helpful.

'I'll take you into the downstairs bathroom, you can clean yourself up a bit, I'll go to your room and get you some fresh clothes.'

'Thanks.'

It was obvious that Donald was quite enjoying my discomfort and was barely able to hold back the laugh he so desperately wanted to release.

'How on earth did you get into this state?' he asked from the other side of the bathroom door as I removed my spoilt clothes.

'From down at the old jetty on the beach behind the church.' I placed the last of my soiled clothes into a laundry bag and handed it back outside to the butler, protecting my modesty at all times, you understand, by hiding behind the bath towel collected thankfully from the heated rail in the large white marble annexed bathroom.

'What were you doing down there? It's not been used for years!'

'Just curious,' I replied, jumping into the shower. Through the rushing water, I heard Donald leave. I resolved to enjoy the hot water of the shower and not to mention the fleece to Judy.

Later, dressed casually and back in the kitchen with a calmer Mary, Donald and I chatted over a steaming, thick creamy and sweet coffee.

As it transpired, Donald was a student of the same Aikido teachings as myself and as Mary washed my clothes for me, Donald and I exchanged notes on tournaments and techniques.

I found it difficult to conceive that this man could be involved in any way, in the theft of Dunning's guns, and the 'The Butler Did It' solution was quickly falling apart.

Feeling much more relaxed and refreshed after the nice hot shower, and coffee with Donald and his beautiful but irrational wife, Donald and I went up the servants' stairs in to the house proper.

'So what happened with the burglary the other day?' I asked as we climbed the stairs.

'Lord Dunning doesn't want us to discuss the matter,' replied Donald. 'He gets very angry about anyone talking about it.'

'Yes, I know, but you know how he feels about me. Believe me when I say the feeling is more than mutual, I'm not going to say anything, and I may be able to shed a little light on the matter.'

Donald looked around suspiciously and then beckoned me close to him in a conspiratorial fashion, then in a low voice he said, 'There was something quite odd about the whole thing really.'

'Odd? How?' I asked.

'Well, normally Mary and myself are here seven days a week, though when Lord Dunning is here it does seem to be a lot longer.'

'I know exactly what you mean.' I sighed.

We reached the balcony and turned up the corridor towards my room. 'You were saying,' I prompted.

'Oh yes. Well, as I was saying, Mary and I are usually here every day. But last Wednesday, Lady Dunning needed to go to the mainland and suggested that Mary go with her.'

'Nothing odd in that,' I answered failing to see the relevance. My father had said it many times over the years, it was always the same with police work, members of the public believing they had vital information that would crack the case wide open, turned out to be groundless hearsay, prejudice and malice and was really the witnesses' preconception of what they believed had possibly happened and to them, proved beyond any doubt the guilt of the person they knew had done it, because the guilty person's eyes were too close together or the guilty felon didn't bathe every day, as normal people did.

I thought Donald was about to give me unwanted proof of my father's theory.

'Ah, but Mark was already on the mainland, being sent to get further supplies for this weekend's party.'

'So?'

'So, her ladyship asked me to pilot the launch, I mean, I've worked here on the island for Lord and Lady Dunning for the last six years, and this is something she has never asked me to do before.' He said it as if that explained everything.

'And that was unusual because...' I again prompted looking blankly at him to which he shrugged, took a deep breath and added:

'Normally, as a matter of course, there is someone in the house or the grounds. But on this one occasion, when the groundsman is ill, Mark is away on the mainland doing chores for Lady Dunning, who then takes both Mary and myself with her, the opportunist house breaker comes across to the island, on the off chance that the house is unoccupied, and lo and behold he's right. And on top of this,' he continued, 'because Lady Dunning had forgotten to set the alarm; arrive back, to find the window in the study wide open, the latches broken, and the alarm has not gone off.'

'In the study?' I asked clarifying what he had just told me.

'Yes.'

'Where the arms locker is?'

'Yes.' There was a pause for several seconds as the dawn of realisation broke over his face. This was quickly replaced by raised eyebrows and a curious glare, suspicion radiating across his brow as he looked at me, his facial muscles working overtime. 'How did you know about that?' he finally asked, the glare of suspicion not receding in the slightest.

'Hey, Donald, I'm a criminologist, I get to find these things out.' He didn't seem to buy this explanation so, reluctantly I added, 'Okay, so his Lordship showed me this morning when we got the shotguns.' This explanation seemed to satisfy him somewhat, but I couldn't help notice the icy stare I was still receiving. 'Anyway,' I continued, attempting to get back on a level footing with him, 'what did you do?' By now we had reached the bedroom door.

'Well, Lady Dunning telephoned the police and I checked the house, just in case our visitor was still about.'

'Okay, so who noticed the missing weapon?'

'Lady Dunning, she must have checked whilst I was out of the room, because when I returned, the bookcase was closed and she told me there had been a theft from the firearms locker.'

'How long did it take you to search the house?'

'Well, it was only a cursory search you understand, I just

checked the rooms from the doorway as I passed, it only took half an hour or so.'

'Okay, Donald, so the police arrived and searched the place properly?'

'Yes, about three quarters of an hour later.'

'What did they come up with?'

'Not a lot really, the glass from the broken window was all over the flower beds and lawn, just outside the window itself and they found some muddy footprints on the carpet and a few shards of glass on the rug.'

'That it?' I asked, expecting a little bit more to go on than that.

'Yes, that's it.'

'Great. Oh well, thanks a lot, it's certainly something to think about.' I sighed somewhat dejectedly.

'Why?' he asked as he started to turn away. 'Why did you want to know all this for anyway, I thought you hated his Lordship.'

'Oh, I do,' I replied honestly. 'I'm just bored. I need something to get my mind around. I thought that the burglary may have been a challenging distraction, that's all. Donald, just before you disappear, did anything else unusual happen last week?'

Donald stopped and turned back to me, he remained silent for several seconds, probably thinking through the previous seven days, his face a mask of pure concentration.

He shook his head, 'No, not as far as I'm aware, Lord Dunning wrote a strongly worded letter to the distillery.' He laughed softly as he recalled the incident.

'Distillery?'

'Yes, he buys his whisky direct from the distillery in Perthshire, that's the only out of the ordinary thing that I can think of other than the burglary.'

'So why did he write the letter? Overcharged or short measured?'

'No, he just said it had an unusual bitter taste and that it was off.'

'Off?'

'Yes, apparently Lady Dunning had ordered a special batch as a celebration of his winning the court case about the paternity.'

'Oh.'

'Yes, Lord Dunning was quite pleased, he said it was a nice gesture and he cracked open a bottle when it arrived, but he said it tasted funny, he refused to drink it and so wrote the letter and returned the rest of the case.'

'What, not serving it to his guests,' I quipped.

'No, Lady Dunning had me to take the unopened bottles back when we went to the mainland on Wednesday, she disposed of the opened bottle.'

'Expensive?' I asked. I wondered just how much Lady Dunning was pleased to find out about her husband's alleged infidelities.

'Very,' Donald nodded. 'About one hundred and fifty pounds a bottle, Pavulon Whisky she called it.'

I whistled in awe of the price. 'Jesus, at one hundred and fifty pounds a bottle, no wonder he wrote a strongly worded letter.'

Donald nodded and turned away.

I closed the door behind him and, kicking my shoes off collapsed on to the bed, thinking about events so far.

It was near to five in the evening when I heard a gentle knocking at my bedroom door. I was lying back on the large comfortable bed, insulated by the reams of student's papers and theses that were strewn all about me, in my well practised and experienced manner of organised chaos.

I dragged myself up from the bed and called, 'Yes, come.'

The door opened cautiously and slowly as Judy entered. I realised then, I had not seen her for nearly twelve hours, she still looked beautiful, even if a little tired.

I greeted her with a gentle kiss.

'Hi,' she sighed, pulling away from my embrace and staring at my bed, complete with partially marked papers. 'Cole! You promised!'

I realised I need not answer, I was caught red handed, I had no excuse, I was guilty and we both knew it.

'Er…sorry,' was all I could really say. I tried to look pitiful – I don't think it worked.

Again I considered working on my lost puppy look. Cute was definitely the way to go in these situations. I just didn't do cute very well.

'What have you been doing all day?' I asked, trying quickly to show that I cared about her.

'Well, first thing this morning, I met Mark and went to see his mother in the village, we had a bite of breakfast and then I met my mother on the quayside for a shopping trip back on the mainland, mother and daughter type stuff you know.'

At the mention of Mark's name, I impressed myself that I kept my composure, I really did trust her, it was him I didn't trust, he was a bloke, and being one, I knew how his mind worked.

'Good shopping trip?'

'No, not really,' she sighed.

I made a space on the bed for her to sit beside me by gently sweeping my arm across the counterpane, collecting and scattering the papers all about. She collapsed wearily on to the bed and I sat myself down next to her, close and reassuringly.

'Want to talk about it?'

'Not really a lot to talk about.' She then began to explain that her mother had visited the family solicitors; Holliday, Carpenter and Drax, a well established law firm in the mainland harbour district. After a lengthy meeting, Lady Dunning had then disappeared to do her own thing, but Judy knew that her mother had spent the day with a man, leaving Judy to wander around the shops all alone.

She had spent a fortune and was still feeling pretty low. I realised then that it must have been a really bad day and was now dreading the end of the month when my flexible friend became a very inflexible fiend.

Judy explained that the party guests were arriving about seven that evening, it was a black tie affair and she needed the time to get ready. She made her excuses and left me alone with my thoughts.

The church clock tower chimed six as I sat in the dimly lit room, I had an hour before being dragged out and paraded in front of Lord Dunning's stuffy business associates, from the world of the chinless wonders.

From experience, I knew that there was no way on this earth or fuller's that Judy would ever be ready in just an hour. Still, I felt obliged to keep my end of the bargain, after all, if I were late I would lose the right to criticise Judy in the future. I saw this as an opportunity to gather some more much needed ammo in the ongoing sex war.

Judy had obtained for me a penguin suit similar to Donald's; it was nice and well fitted. Reluctantly I had to admit to myself as I looked into the full length mirror in the corner of the room, that I filled it out well and did look damn good too. Still, I did feel sorry for Donald, who had to dress like this all the time.

In fancy dress like this, it looked great. Very smart and sexy, and with any luck, Judy would think so too. But dressing like this all the time was just too damn ridiculous for words.

After a great deal of self-preening and self-admiration, I decided that I was as ready as I was ever going to be.

Somewhere across the not too distant night sky, the church bells tolled the hour of seven.

The guests had all arrived and I could hear the sound of excited conversation emanating from somewhere downstairs, I presumed it would be the drawing room.

I pulled back the curtains of the large windows of my room and looked out into the darkness beyond, rain was gently pattering against the glass pane as the heavens once more released their frustrations on the island. I stared across the sprawling vista of the Dunning estate, the intensity of the rain increasing and the gentle droplets now hammered down against the window.

The whole atmosphere of the impending evening, the howling wind and the driving rain had a depressing effect upon me, I was here, someplace I did not wish to be, in weather that was particularly unpleasant, with people I either didn't know or didn't like, Judy, of course was the only exception, and because I loved her, I forced myself to cope, to endure and to enjoy it.

Inside, I felt even more out of place than previously.

It was a quarter past the hour, according to Mickey, who as always was patiently sitting passing the time on my left wrist. With Judy on my other arm looking radiant as ever, we walked down the staircase together, into the hallway and towards the hooray henrys.

On entering the drawing room, I only recognised Lady Dunning. Lord Dunning the host and master of the evening was nowhere to be seen.

In the absence of her father, whilst Lady Dunning laughed and guffawed with the socialites, Judy led me around the room.

I was first of all introduced to a Stephen Carpenter, I soon discovered, that he was the lawyer appointed to be executor of Lord Dunning's will, in the unlikely event of something unfortunate happening to him. Carpenter was, it transpired, the partner of the local law firm, Holliday, Carpenter and Drax, he had been a friend of the Dunnings for the last ten years and Lord Dunning it appeared had put an awful lot of business his firm's way.

Carpenter was a giant of a man, over six feet tall, but slim, bordering on emaciation, he had the appearance that a strong breeze would break him in half. Although of a pleasant and engaging disposition, his head looked too large and heavy, oversized for his thin scrawny neck. His clothes, despite being neat, tidy and obviously very expensive and tailor-made, seemed to hang limply off him. His eyes were dull and grey, his rough face pock-marked by a juvenile case of chicken pox. Listening to him speak was difficult, as he seemed to be speaking with a sock in his mouth, which, as it turned out, was not far from the truth.

His lips, I noticed, were a brilliant red and at first I thought he might be wearing lipstick, however, I soon realised the cause of his full scarlet lips as he was constantly dabbing at his mouth, mopping up and wiping away little drops and flecks of blood.

'Are you all right?' I asked, genuine concern for this elderly man, seventy if he was a day.

'Yes, fine thank you.' He smiled, his yellow brown crooked teeth smeared with blood. 'I had a wisdom tooth removed earlier today, I shouldn't have come but Helen was most insistent.' He dabbed again.

'Close friend of the family are you?' I asked and handed him a fresh napkin that he accepted with a nodded thanks. 'Of Martin's, yes.' He dabbed, 'But Helen and I have had a bit of a falling out I'm afraid.'

'I'm sorry to hear that.'

'Yes, and all because of that new will of his.' He made a quick intake of breath and shuddered violently.

'Are you sure you're all right?'

'Just a little post-operative pain.'

I saw Lady Dunning looking across at us, a forced smile, that of the unhappy hostess making the best of a bad job, painted immobile on her face. I caught her attention and she was over in a flash.

I explained Stephen's discomfort and asked for something to help him with the pain.

'Oh, you poor thing, I should never have insisted you attend, I'm awfully sorry.' Lady Dunning quickly put her arm around him in sympathy. 'Stephen, why don't you go up to bed, I'll ask Donald to bring you up something for the pain, something to help you sleep.'

He nodded his acceptance, bade his goodnights and was quickly and quietly ushered out of the room with Lady Dunning.

Judy clutched my elbow and gently steered me towards the next person on her society must meet list.

Mr Henry Stanford was shorter than myself by a good four inches, something which immediately improved my own self-esteem, he was broadly built, looking something akin to one of the old children's toys which were impossible to knock down, he peered back at me through deeply recessed bloodshot eyes. From my vantage point, looking down upon him, I could not help but notice that his short, dark hair was worn in the 'centre parted by Moses' style, however, vanity or a dare had encouraged him to wear a toupee to hide this fact. Over the years, I have to come to view hairpieces in three distinct groupings.

Firstly there is the: Is that a toupee? class. Secondly the: That is a toupee! class, and thirdly, there is the final: What the hell is that! class.

Unfortunately Stanford's wig was definitely in the third category. It was matted and worn in patches, threadbare in others. The whole hairpiece flapped when he moved, exposing tantalising flashes of sun-starved pinky white flesh beneath. It was supposed to draw onlookers' attention away from the fact that the wearer was follically challenged. But this was like an optical magnet, I found my eyes constantly drawn to it.

Stanford was a crashing bore, he constantly jabbered on about the textile manufacturing industry from the north of Yorkshire, an industry he wasted no time in telling me all about. He spoke with a melodic, hypnotic and soft Yorkshire accent. Stanford, I discovered, was here with his business partner, Brian Drake, who I saw was wrapping himself expertly around a bottle of Lord Dunning's finest malt whisky.

Judy noticed my eyes straying to Stanford's hairpiece every time he tried to draw me into conversation about the dying textile trade, and she saved me from making a complete ass of myself by pointing me towards Drake.

Drake was a thickset Eastender who spoke with a heavy, deep Cockney accent and who I half expected to burst into song about chimney sweeps and Mary Poppins at any minute, which, thankfully he never did. The first thing anyone noticed about Brian was his hair, regardless of what he did to it, it always returned to a wild, chaotic, untamed, wiry mess. Jet-black, his face was shrouded beneath the entangled hair and his uncontrolled full beard and moustache. You got the impression that you were talking to a hairy ball, every so often though, he would blink and give you a focal point of where his eyes were located. When he spoke, the thick London accent came tripping through the mass of hair and was greatly muffled by the experience, some would say thankfully.

He too spoke with regret about the decline of his industry and the role land developers were taking in his downfall. He seemed to be taking it personally and the effect of the whisky was more than enough to make him broodier and more sullen as the evening progressed. I made my excuses and was next introduced to Miss Jayne Frobisher.

Tall, slim and perfectly proportioned, her long blonde hair trailed down her back to just below her waist, her skin, alabaster white, pure clear and unblemished. Her eyes clear and bright sapphire blue, her full pouting lips, red to match the cocktail dress she wore so provocatively. A long split to the top of her thigh and the wide-open back showing that the dress fitted only where it touched.

Not that I was paying that much attention, you understand.

She had an hourglass figure for which many women would kill, most probably their husbands.

It turned out that she was in fact Lord Dunning's former private secretary; she had worked for him when he was a government minister. She was very pleasant to talk to with her soft harmonious voice and deep, enchanting and sensual, intelligent eyes.

Judy saw the look in my eyes, the half-dreamlike look that drifted across my face, but before I could pursue any conversation with this angelic creature, she dragged me away to meet another of the weekend guests.

Major Forsythe and his wife the honourable Lady Forsythe were next on my social circuit. He looked and behaved like a pompous idiot, a man who had obviously got to the top of his profession by referring to Daddy's bank account and his wife's chapter in de Bretts. He was a loud man with a neat, thinly trimmed moustache and a delicate golden monocle, very suave looking in his army dress uniform, he appeared ungainly and gangly as he moved, his stature belying his unquestionable fitness.

A Major in the seventh Royal Horse Artillery, he appeared well tanned, his dark eyes showing a cunning intelligence and undoubtedly a rapier like strategic mind.

'You look well, sir,' I said, extending my right hand in friendship. The army man looked me up and down quizzingly, making no attempt to clasp the hand offered to him.

'Yes.' He took a swig from the tumbler in his hand. 'You the teacher chap?'

'A lecturer,' I corrected, this was becoming a habit. I withdrew my hand.

'Those who can, do!' he began.

'Those who can't, teach,' I sighed. Completing the statement for him, obviously written by one of the 'do' brigade.

'That's it,' he nodded. Obviously impressed that I knew the wise words of which he was so eloquently speaking.

'Been overseas?' I was trying to make at least one friend here. Judy kept nudging me in the ribs, encouraging me to persevere with this man. I felt she was taking my love for her to new-found extremes.

'Belize!' he nodded.

'In America?'

'Are there others? You teacher chaps should know that. Must dash, other people to meet!' And with that he was gone.

I released a great sigh of relief and watched him leave.

As he walked around the room to the other groups, I noticed he walked with a slight, barely perceptible limp, probably injured during a full contact cocktail party somewhere, or possibly shrapnel from an overdone vol-au-vent catching him unawares. The scene played out in my mind.

Judy instinctively knew something was going on in there as she jabbed me hard in the ribs with her elbow when she saw me smiling inanely.

The honourable Lady Gwendolyne Forsythe, on the other hand was a real charmer. Her naturally silvery hair was chemically enhanced to its current auburn state, her face, heavily wrinkled and aged beyond her sixty years by careless sun worship in her formative years. Her dress was immaculate, and despite her twenty or so years seniority over her husband, it was obvious by the way her eyes followed him around the room she loved him deeply.

The many jewels that were draped so tastefully and enthusiastically about her arms and neck appeared to be worth, on average, at least as much as my car and probably a little more than my flat. I was vaguely aware that I was drooling openly as the estimations and calculations were done in my head.

Upon speaking to Lady Forsythe, I found her to be a very down-to-earth person, maternal, pleasant and instantly likeable.

She knew that she had been born rich, and she appreciated the fact that other people had not been as fortunate. She had made a decision, growing up and maturing that she would do her part in redressing the balance. Despite her advancing years, she was wild and knew how to enjoy herself, she was not stuffy or pretentious, I liked her.

'How was Belize?' I asked, pouring her a drink from a nearby decanter.

'Too hot for me. Alan went, I stayed at home. Much more fun. We have a young gardener you know.' She giggled and gave me a knowing wink.

As we walked away from her, Judy whispered to me that she thought that Major Forsythe was the man she had seen her mother with earlier in the day in Marlbury Port. I glanced across my shoulder at the major.

Lady Dunning had returned and seemed to be ignoring him and, to be fair, he appeared to be doing the same to her.

Now, Lady Beatrice Barton, the next socialite on Judy's hit list, was what you would expect from someone born with a silver spoon in her mouth. The first thing you noticed about her was the strong smell of lavender and peppermints that hung in the air like a swarm about ten feet around her. Her white hair piled high on her head in a beehive style matched her pearls and she incessantly spoke about Bopsey, her ever so pampered French poodle.

'Hello, Lady Barton, my name is Cole.' I sat down beside her on the leather sofa.

'One should wait to be invited before sitting with a lady,' she replied and promptly slapped my wrist with her small, pearl encrusted purse.

'Oh, I'm sorry.' I looked at Judy, smiled and shrugged.

'I only let Bopsey on the seat with me!' she continued, striking me again, this time across the chest.

'Steady on old girl.'

'Old girl! Old girl is it!' I saw the purse coming, eye level and gaining speed. I flinched and forced myself out of its trajectory.

'What the hell is your problem!' I jumped to my feet and turned to face the old woman. The room went quiet as eyes everywhere turned towards us.

'Do not use that tone of voice with me young man. Bopsey never talks to me like that!'

I resisted the temptation to slap her back, barely.

I attempted to correct my initial floundering introduction with the old woman, but found Lady Barton irritating, like an itch you just can't get to, she was eighty going on eighteen and whined and whinged for several minutes, before I eventually gave up and was able to steer Judy away from her.

'Cole, did you really have to?' Judy said, feigning distaste at my escape plan. 'Telling the poor woman you were terminally ill and couldn't afford to talk to her a moment longer, that was very rude.'

'Look Judy, we're all dying, talking to that haggard old witch was bringing on a good case for euthanasia or culling the old folk, believe me.'

Mr and Mrs Simmons were as refreshing to meet as Lady Forsythe. They instantly demanded to be called John and Sylvia. Your typical poor types making it big. They remembered their roots and the struggle, they were proud of their origins. I liked them too, they were my kind of people. John was forty, two years older than Sylvia, his childhood sweetheart. He was a large, rotund man, bubbly and energetic, contrasting with Sylvia's more quiet and reserved nature, they were both fair haired, hers bobbed, his thinning, they looked well suited and, in their respective evening wear, both looked impeccably turned out.

'Cole.' Judy appeared at my side with a man on each arm, one I recognised from the television earlier in the week. He was the journalist who had got to Dunning. The other I did not recognise. 'This is...'

'Tim Wolfe,' I interrupted, extending my hand. The journalist was bigger than I had imagined. Not in the same league as Lord Dunning or any other sumo, but he was of impressive stature. Cuddly, was not a word that I would attach to him, in his presence. His clothes, despite his best efforts, were still unkempt and wrinkled, He eagerly shook my hand.

'You've heard of me?' He smiled as he pumped my arm enthusiastically.

'Yes, of course.'

'Wow, no one usually shakes my hand when they know me.'

He seemed genuinely pleased that I had not tried to hit him with something or refer to his family tree and the unknown location of his father in its branches.

'Everyone expects me to be like I am on TV.' He smiled again, his chipolata fingers released my hand, leaving a wet, slimy residue in their wake. I wiped my hand casually on the back of a nearby chair.

'Hell, just doing your job.'

'That's right,' he beamed. After a few seconds of silence, I got the distinct feeling that his ever roving eyes were measuring me up for a column or two in his paper and I decided to opt for security of speech when near him, just in case.

'Cole, this is Michael Trevalian, a very old family friend.' Judy introduced the second man. She was pleased to see him – that was obvious by the way she used both her arms now to wrap herself around his left arm. She was as pleased to see him as she had been to see Mark, and this started me wondering again.

'Judith, not that old surely.' Trevalian laughed.

'So,' I asked, a mock laugh underneath the question, 'just how well do you know Judith?'

Trevalian, either did not hear the barbed question, or else chose not to rise to the veiled threat, looked down lovingly into her eyes as Judy gazed back into his.

'We were childhood friends, we grew up together,' he replied sighing.

Trevalian was a good five inches taller than myself, short cropped hair, his dark, olive coloured skin revealing his true origins in the eastern part of Europe. His deep-set green eyes on either side of an obviously broken nose encouraged me to believe that he had been a childhood friend of other women and their current partners had reacted in the approved and well documented manner of beating the crap out of him if he overstepped the mark.

Wolfe looked on, obviously entertained by the scene playing out before his very eyes, his next story about to break.

'You working?' I asked coldly, the question bringing him back to reality with an obvious thump.

'Yes I am, and yourself?'

I nodded. 'What do you do?'

'I'm a doctor. My wife and I have just returned from a spell overseas.'

'Your wife?'

'Yes, she couldn't make it tonight, she's on call.'

'Oh.' I realised once again that jealousy was an ever-present danger. I should know better by now.

'Oh indeed,' smiled Wolfe, more to himself than anyone near

us.

'Yes, we've just returned from Columbia and we're now ready to open our own practice in Marlbury Port.'

'What were you doing over there?' I asked, now showing an interest in this no longer threatening male.

'We were working with the World Health Organisation. We did our five years and now we've come home.'

'Doctor Trevalian,' interrupted Wolfe stepping closer to us once more, 'Did you have any involvement in the paternity testing involving Lord Dunning?' As expected, Wolfe fired the question out of the blue and from the hip, it caught the doctor completely off guard.

'Er... Yes. He specifically asked for me to do it, he wanted someone he could trust.'

'And the result was?' Wolfe was leading the unsuspecting doctor down a dangerous path, the Hippocratic oath was pretty explicit about the type of information I knew Wolfe was after.

'I gave the results to Stephen Carpenter. I can't say any more than that.'

And he didn't.

We were laughing and joking and I actually began to enjoy myself. Wolfe, Trevalian, Judy and I were putting the world to rights and having a good time doing it.

Suddenly, and without warning, the atmosphere in the room did a quick one hundred and eight degree shift, the joviality changed, from carefree and happy to anxious and paranoid. Tension spread through the room like a good rumour. The laughter and cheerful conversation that had previously exuded from everyone present, being replaced by a tangible, unwholesome silence.

Without turning to face the door, I knew that Lord Dunning had arrived.

From the little time I had spent with him, I knew that the man could traumatise a carnival with just a whisper of his presence.

The huge gelatinous mound of a man seemed to radiate hate and loathing, it oozed from his every pore and every living thing seemed to send it straight back, he seemed to enjoy this response, a perverted sense of power and he always drew the hate back towards himself, feeding off it.

His dulcet tones ripped through the party like a saw through brittle bones without anaesthetic.

'What the hell are these people doing here!' He was, barely able to maintain his temper.

As I turned to the door, I clearly saw the vein in his forehead throbbing violently.

Even from this vantage point, a good fifteen feet from the blocked door, I felt reassured that I was well protected, just in case the vein burst and we all got sprayed with thick, cholesterol clogged Dunning puss.

From the way Lord Dunning leered menacingly around the room at his guests, his head thrust forward, his almost white, bloodless lips drawn tightly back revealing his apparently too many teeth for that small mean mouth, flecks of white bubbling foam appeared on his chins, oozing slowly down all three of them, pooling on his wide rising and falling chest, I could see he was angry in the extreme. I saw that both of his hands were rhythmically bunched and released alternately forming tight, white knuckled fists and flat slabs of wide, red meat. His breathing was hard and regular and his purple face edging ever darker as his obvious rage deepened.

I don't think he actually expected an answer; it was just his idea of an icebreaker.

Lady Dunning, now topping up her empty tumbler stopped and turned to him, flashing a nervous smile across the room in his direction. 'I invited them, dear.'

The smile she was displaying was obviously false, forced to hide her embarrassment.

I knew how she must be feeling, being put on the spot like that in front of all these people, friends and acquaintances all.

'Well, dear!' He snarled bitterly, sarcasm dripping from every word like an almost tangible venom, 'You can just bloody well uninvite them. I don't want these parasites and back-stabbers in my house, eating from my table or receiving any of my bloody hospitality.' Lord Dunning spat each and every word like it had an evil, bitter taste. I could tell it was something he felt very strongly about, it was obvious that he was a little irritated.

'Cheers.' I raised my glass, a toast in his general direction and smiled.

This only seemed to goad him on and enrage him further.

Can't understand why?

'Get these bloodsuckers out of my house, or I'll bring the dogs in and sort them myself.' Lord Dunning's voice was rising in volume, his tone was almost screaming now as it seemed to pierce the veiled realms of ultrasonics.

'I didn't know you had dogs here,' I whispered to Judy as an aside.

'We don't,' she whispered back, 'that's what Daddy calls the labourers from the village,' she explained. Judy was trembling. I noted that she was genuinely afraid.

'Are you all right?' I hugged her to me. She nodded briefly. Through barely restrained tears she whimpered back, 'I've never seen him so angry.'

To add a little extra atmosphere, during Lord Dunning's ranting and raving, puffing and panting exhibition, demonstrating his displeasure to his wife's choice of weekend house guest; I caught a glimpse of a brilliant electric blue white flash of light through the lightly curtained windows. This was followed almost instantly by a deep resonant rattling, rolling boom that seemed to shake the panes of glass in the windows.

It was a neat trick and I thought that if Dunning had arranged this, he was a better showman than I had ever given him credit for. More thunder rolled heavily with deep, unbridled menace across the heavens.

Somewhere in the rolling darkness behind me, a woman screamed. It scared me to death.

'Sorry, Sylvia hates thunder and lightning.'

I looked across the room to John Simmons, he was now holding his wife's hand tightly, both had taken a position away from the curtained windows and were now standing towards the rear of the room, furthest from the windows, their backs pressed tightly against the solid looking wood panelled walls of the drawing room.

Beside them, I caught a glimpse of Major Forsythe looking at his watch, probably trying to decide whether he could order a driver to collect him and his wife from Marlbury Port harbour at this hour, in such a storm. Although I realised the crossing back would be rather more entertaining in this weather.

Inquisitively, I checked my own watch. It was 7.45.

With his point made, and the special effects of nature punctuating his every word and gesture, Dunning stormed out of the room. He slammed the heavy wooden panel doors behind him with such force that a neat glass vase on the table beside the door was shaken from its position. Falling effortlessly from its plinth, the vase shattered loudly as it struck the carpeted floor. Flowers and water spewed across the deep, plush carpet. Upstairs, almost in unison, another sound of smashing glass erupted in sympathy.

'Excitable isn't he,' I commented to Tim Wolfe who was now standing next to Judy and myself. He nodded silently and took another hard slug of whisky from the tumbler he clutched so fiercely.

John Simmons nodded, 'Certainly is.' He crossed the room to join us, escorting his nervous wife. 'I don't know why Lady Dunning invited any of us here to be honest. She knows how that miserable sod feels about us.'

'You don't' like him?' I asked sitting down next to where Sylvia had been directed. John passed her a near full tumbler of sherry that she accepted with both hands, smiling her gratitude to her loving husband.

'No, I think he hates everyone here passionately. And from what the others were saying before you came down, I think you'll find that everyone here hates him at least twice as much back.'

'What, such a likeable chap as good old Lord Dunning, mister personality himself, certainly not,' I replied sarcastically.

'Mister personality *disorder* perhaps,' interjected Sylvia, putting her tumbler down on the occasional table next to where she was now sitting.

'Why is that?' I asked.

'I don't think it's for me to comment on really,' said John. 'Well,' he added after a few seconds thought, 'I can't really say anything about how or why the others feel what they do, but for Sylvia and myself, it's personal.'

'Go on.'

'That bastard drove my little girl to kill herself.'

It was incredulous; I could hardly believe what I was hearing. I could imagine Lord Dunning giving someone a nervous complex, but to drive him or her to suicide, this seemed a little too much for me to comprehend.

'How on earth did he manage to do that?' I continued.

'My daughter, Lucy, was at that very encouragable age.'

'How old was she?'

'Seventeen, she was very vulnerable to thoughts and ideas presented to her by vindictive, evil and twisted minds like Dunning's,' he explained. 'Anyway, Lucy was influenced very much by money.'

'How long ago was this?'

'Five years, at that time in our lives, we had only just got the company going, so money in our house was not that easy to come by and was not easily available.'

'How did she meet him?'

'Lucy had won a scholarship to go to university; I mean we couldn't afford for her to go otherwise. She met Dunning at one of those society dinners that they put on at university these days, guest speakers and suchlike.'

I nodded the fact that I was familiar with the evenings he was talking about. This did not seem to register with him and I could tell from the expression on his face, head back, cocked at an angle, his eyes distracted looking upward, that he was seeing the incident again in his mind's eye.

'I do know the evenings you mean,' I finally said, encouraging him to continue with his narration.

He snapped out of his self-induced trance, shaking his head to remove the images he was still seeing.

'Well, something happened that night, there was a big drugs scandal, Dunning greased the right palms and all of a sudden, he wasn't even at the party, his name vanishing from all the guest lists.'

'How do you know?'

'I have it on very good authority that, sometime during the night, Dunning gave my daughter some controlled substance or other. It was some designer drug, Lucy was instantly addicted.'

'What was it?'

He shrugged, 'I don't know, the autopsy was inconclusive.'

'I'm so sorry. What actually happened?' I did not wish to pry into the family's grief, but the way both John and Sylvia were looking at each other, I could tell that both wished their story to be told.

'She died three years ago last October. She became a totally different person, not my little girl anymore, I saw her the day before she hung herself, she didn't even know who I was.'

'Without forensic evidence or proof of the drug, what have you done to support your case?'

'For the last two years, Sylvia and I have been pursuing a civil case about the cover-up at the university. I'd be prepared to swing for that bastard after what he has done to my family. Lucy was our only child. Now all this business success is for nothing. We've used all the money we've earned to fund our court battle, perhaps one day the truth will come out. But people like Dunning ruin lives and are never brought to task for it.'

Michael Trevalian who had been sitting quietly in the corner of the room listening to what John had been saying, suddenly broke the silence.

'Excuse me, perhaps I can offer my help.' He sat forward, leaning his slim towering frame forward.

'How?' John looked back towards the tall, cosmopolitan doctor.

'Working in South America, I came across many drugs and poisons, perhaps I can review the medical records, I might find something the doctors here weren't looking for.'

'You think they might have missed something?' John appeared to brighten, expectation and hope replacing the melancholy and grief displayed only minutes earlier.

'I can't promise anything,' Trevalian acknowledged, putting both hands up in defence and sitting further back in the leather chair, 'but I do know quite a lot about unusual drugs and natural poisons, it became a bit of a speciality in Columbia I'm afraid.'

'Thank you, Michael, anything you can do to help, we would appreciate.'

Trevalian nodded and looked back towards the window.

Wolfe looked at him, long and hard, his eyes narrowing as he surveyed this larger than life Good Samaritan.

Despite John's comments, I detected an awful lot of well restrained anger and hatred in his eyes as he related his story. John and Sylvia held hands and comforted each other. I could see they hated Dunning with a passion. It was an ingredient for a great party.

Judy, who had been standing next to me, had heard all this. I knew it would be difficult for her to understand how her loving father could be perceived by others to be this evil, manipulative monster, yet she said nothing in his defence, almost as if, deep down inside, she knew they were right.

Major and Lady Forsythe came over to join our little throng as the party seemed to try and work itself back up into a half-hearted frenzy of general lethargy.

Certainly John and Sylvia Simmons had lost all interest in the party and were now hugging each other tightly for mutual support on the couch. They were not happy campers.

'Damn fiery sort of chap,' commented the major, ignoring the emotional carnage of the Simmons with what I interpreted as being professional and much practised ease, no trace of emotion in his voice.

I found his brash callousness and lack of emotional under-standing to be extremely disturbing.

'I'm sorry! What the hell do you mean, fiery?' It was not a question I required an answer for, but the major offered one anyway.

'Lord Dunning. Damn fiery. Causing a scene. Damn poor show that.' The major spoke in short clipped sentences, each with no emotion His narrow, pencilled moustache twitching with every word.

I rated Major Forsythe a clear eleven plus on a scale of one to ten of the most irritating people I had ever had the misfortune to encounter. His jet-black moustache and short-cropped hair were stuck rigidly in place by the application of several pounds of Brylcream.

He reminded me of the typical upper class military type por-trayed so vividly on Saturday afternoon Second World War films, a squadron leader at the very least.

What the kindly and intelligent Lady Forsythe saw in the major was unknown to me, a woman like that could surely not be attracted to the man's status and position in society. To me, I considered him a repulsive vile little man, slimy and cold. Even though he was taller in stature than myself, I still considered him a weasel. And to top it all, I really didn't like him either.

Above the now near continuous thunderclaps, the barely audible church bells tolled the hour of eight.

Lady Dunning had done a wonderful PR job on the house-guests, and despite Lord Dunning's best efforts to scupper the party earlier, she had managed to persuade everyone to try and eat him out of house and home.

Although not back to its previously raucous level of joviality, the party guests were warming to the idea of taking advantage of Dunning's unoffered and openly resented hospitality, if he didn't like it, tough.

We left the drawing room, crossing the main hallway to the dining room, only the major did not accompany us, he made his excuses.

'Be with you shortly, urgent phone call to make.'

Lady Forsythe called after him, 'Don't be long, Alan.'

'Not to worry, dear.'

I imagined that he probably needed to reorder his supply of Brylcream for breakfast in the morning.

Lord Dunning had joined us. His wife had worked some magic on him too, his ranting and raving had been adequately subdued.

Donald stood stiffly to almost regimental attention near the hallway door, beside the long sideboard. He was watching Lady Dunning attentively, awaiting the order to begin serving the huge meal Mary had so laboriously prepared.

Because of Lord Dunning's presence, needless to say conversation was a little stilted and dull.

Major Forsythe rejoined us about fifteen minutes later; he was completely drenched, except for his hair, the Brylcream a highly effective water repellent.

'Major! Are you all right?' Lady Dunning rose from her chair and crossed the room to him as he staggered in, bedraggled and leaving a pool of water on the carpet at his feet.

'Yes, thank you. I'm sorry I'm in such a state, not good show really. Could I go upstairs and freshen up?'

'Why yes, yes of course you can,' replied Lady Dunning and signalled Donald to help the major to his room.

Lord Dunning slammed his cutlery harshly down on to the table, an assortment of knives, forks and spoons scattering with the impact.

'The hell it is!' He pushed the chair back from the table and rose to his feet.

'Oh no, not again,' I sighed under my breath.

Lady Barton who, by some quirk of fate, was sitting beside me leant across and whispered conspiratorially, 'Don't worry, dear, he's always been the same, spoilt little brat I'm afraid, turned him into a spoilt big brat, Bopsey has always disliked him.'

'What happened Major? How did you get to be so wet?' asked Judy turning to look at the sodden soldier. Her tone was blunt, flat and filled with suspicion it was obvious to me that she was not really interested in anything the man had to say for himself.

I smiled to myself. I knew he was wet when we first met.

Lady Dunning obviously caught the tone in her daughters voice and the hidden suggestion in her question as she spun around and snapped at her daughter. 'Judith!' It was a warning shot across the bows from mother to daughter and both parties knew it.

'No. It's all right. You need to know anyway. I'm afraid we can't get a launch back until the morning. I have just spoken to my valet, he is staying in one of the bed and breakfast places on the harbour back in Marlbury, and he has just informed me that there will be no seagoing traffic from there until the morning, due to the weather and heightened storm warnings.'

The major turned to Lady Forsythe and said more to her than anyone, although we could all hear clearly, 'I have to report to my commanding officer tomorrow afternoon, I've been posted to Ireland on Monday to cover the troop withdrawals.'

'Oh no!' gasped Lady Forsythe. I couldn't believe it; she really did have feelings for the odious little creep.

'Yes, I'm afraid so, dear. I was upset too about the news. I'm being sent to replace Major Matthews, he was killed in a mine clearing operation this afternoon.'

Lady Forsythe looked a little worried, a deep frown slicing across her forehead as she asked, 'Are you all right?'

'I was very concerned about this and went outside to clear my head.'

'Not like Belize then?' she asked, a tremble in her voice causing the jewels draped around her neck to shimmer in the flickering gaslight of the room.

He shook his head, 'But just as I got out on to the patio, I saw a man loitering near to the rose garden. I called out to him and he just took off. I gave chase but he had too great a lead on me and I lost him in the dark.'

'Did you recognise him?' Wolfe jumped to his feet, an impressive achievement in acknowledgement of his bulk, it was also highly entertaining, his waistline seeming to have a life of its own and centrifugal force acting independently on its great mass. 'Quick, let's go and see if we can find him, he may be the thief from the other night.'

I looked round to see who else was willing to undertake the quest with him when I felt Judy's gently restraining hand on my arm, I nodded to her and called across the table to the excited news hound.

'Tim, if he is the thief from the other night, he may have the gun with him.' The restraining hand on my arm increased its pressure, advising me strongly that staying here with her was the better of the two options.

It was a sobering thought and all heroic inclinations were instantly and happily swept away, dismissed and forgotten as Wolfe retook his seat at the dinner table.

'Er… Yes… Good point Meredith, thank you for pointing that out.'

'How about calling the police?' I eventually suggested. I glanced down at Mickey sat patiently on my left wrist, it was 8.20.

'Don't you bloody bunch of ingrates worry yourselves, I'll bloody do it!' Lord Dunning was on his feet again, striding angrily to the door, 'accidentally' bumping the major with his shoulder, the major rocking on his heels under the impact of the much larger mass. 'I want to see that thieving bastard strung up. And while I'm on, I'll make arrangements for these bloody freeloading bastards to be shifted off my island!'

The door slammed shut behind him and I knew Lord Dunning had not calmed down.

Lady Dunning was on her feet now, nimbly crossing the room, 'Darling, can I have a word with you please.' She opened the hastily closed door behind her swiftly retreating husband. Lady Dunning's statement was simply that, her tone ensured that it could not be mistaken for a question or a suggestion.

On reflection, this was the only occasion I could recall, in all the time I had known Lady Dunning to use any term of endearment to her dear spouse. Out in the hallway I saw Lord Dunning stop, his great frame turning to face his wife, and then my view was sliced closed as the door, finally, eased to behind them.

Lord Dunning's enraged reply, 'Now?'

'Yes, in the study, please.' Lady Dunning's soft, reasonable response was in total contrast to the hostility in her husband's demeanour.

Through the now closed door, I heard Lord Dunning release a great sigh of resignation. Lord Dunning's heavy, hollow footfalls could be heard crossing the cold hard marble floor of the hallway.

Lady Dunning's voice echoed back, presumably to us, her house guests, 'Won't be long.' Then she too was heard tip tapping away.

'Happy families?' I whispered to Judy.

She appeared to take no notice of me though, she was staring straight at Major Forsythe, her eyes narrowed and fixed in what I can only describe as an openly hostile way. In turn, the major had obviously felt the daggers from Judy and was visibly nervous under her withering incessant glare.

Once more, conversation was scarce; Lord Dunning had had an impact yet again.

Topics ranging from the weather to the current state of the economy were broached briefly, only to quickly run out of steam.

Wolfe I noticed, neglected to offer any views, he sat, impassively in stony silence, watching, listening to the interaction of the diners. Like a social sponge, he was submitting all to memory. His eyes across the table met mine and he smiled slyly in acknowledgement, he knew that I had recognised his people watching game.

To open the conversation again, I mentioned briefly my favourite soap opera on television and immediately wished I had thought of something more intelligent to say, as the conversation instantly swung way to the left and the state of education of today's youth leapt to the fore, uniting the clutch of opinionated diners.

Only Judy, Wolfe and Trevalian remained silent, as the barbed discussion picked up momentum and vitriolic accusation, mounting unwarranted faults and failings on my profession continued unabated. By the time the topic turned on to teachers' pay and their hours and holidays I was in desperate need of a breath of fresh air.

'Judy, let's go outside for a bit, shall we?' I grabbed Judy's hand and half-dragged her from the room.

We left the stuffy dining room and the other guests who had now found a topic of universal harmony. They seemed to have forgotten their own agendas and were happy to complain to each other about the failings of our education system.

I felt really pleased that my chosen profession was so well thought of by this section of the population.

'Why have you brought me out here?' Judy stared at me, totally oblivious to the comments being made about both our careers.

'I thought that the other guests would like some more time to complete their character assassination of me,' I replied, realising for the first time, the whole topic of conversation had gone totally over Judy's head. Obviously something else had her complete attention and I imagined that I knew which of the moustache-wearing guests it was.

As we passed the closed study door, all hell seemed to be suddenly let loose behind it.

Simultaneously, as the church bells tolled the arrival of eight thirty, it was accompanied by the near sound of glass shattering and a terror-stricken scream tearing through the night.

Being a nosy person by choice more than by design, I turned and ran to the closed door of the study. Grabbing the handle, I twisted it and forcefully pushed the door into the room, the door swinging back easily.

The scene that greeted me made the contents of my stomach do a cartwheel and it was all I could do to keep the contents from making a rapid, projected exit. I felt glad that as yet we had not eaten.

Judy had followed me into the room close by my right elbow. She peeked around me curiously and then she screamed as only a woman can.

Three hundred decibels plus, straight down my right ear. So now, I had not only rising and insistent nausea to deal with, but deafness too.

A hysterical daughter and a mother, already in the room, on her knees in the middle of the study, her head held in both hands as she stared towards the study windows, gibbering inanely and rocking rapidly back and forth, obviously in a state of deep shock.

Lord Dunning on the other hand was going to be easier to deal with, a lot easier; after all, it was him everyone was screaming at.

He had been shot and he was going to stay well and truly shot for quite a while yet to come judging by the red violent mess which was oozing incessantly out of his chest, it spilled out all over the large ornate desk in front of him.

A few seconds elapsed, the time distorted into uneventful hours, when Major Forsythe hobbled into the room behind Judy and myself.

'My God! What on earth happened here?' He surveyed the scene and noted the remains of Lord Dunning.

'What does it look like?' I snapped back. 'You think maybe his Papermate burst?'

Sarcasm, Judy is always telling me, is the lowest form of wit, but I regard it as the highest form of intelligence, anyway, it's a defence mechanism, I always use to de-stress myself.

Seeing the look he gave me, I realised he was about to make some response, I knew it would not be appropriate and would only serve to upset Judy and her mother further. I quickly added,

'Please, take Lady Dunning and Judy back into the dining room, I'll be with you shortly.'

The major seemed only too happy to oblige, nodding quickly in acknowledgement; he carefully scooped up the gibbering wreck which was Lady Dunning and escorted her out of the study and away from the carnage, Judy followed of her own accord, lost and bewildered, like a lost sheep she followed whoever she was instructed to.

Donald, Trevalian and Wolfe quickly appeared in the hallway, running past the open study door; alerted no doubt by the sudden screams and sounds of smashing glass. They appeared to be making their way to the drawing room but, when their combined attention was drawn to me in the study, they stopped and came over to me.

'What happened?' asked Wolfe breathing hard, his unfit body already perspiring after his ten-metre dash.

'He's been shot!' Trevalian was at my side in a heartbeat. Quickly, professionally he examined Lord Dunning for signs of life.

'Michael, don't move anything,' I warned.

Trevalian nodded his understanding.

'Donald,' I continued, 'can you keep everyone out of here for a few minutes?'

'Yes, what are you going to do?'

'I want to have a quick look round. Get Mary to alert the authorities, Lord Dunning has been seriously injured, it doesn't look good.' I looked back to the obvious corpse of the lord, sitting in his high back chair, his chest and upper torso spilling its contents out on to the desktop.

'Is he all right?' Concern for his employer was very touching.

'No, not really,' I replied, making a call based on common sense and basic anatomy. 'I think he's dead.'

Trevalian nodded and stepped away from Lord Dunning, 'Sure is,' he quickly confirmed.

'Of course, right, yes. Mary to call the police, me to keep everyone out of your way, got it.' Donald left in somewhat of a daze, pulling the door closed behind him as he went to carry out my requests.

So, here I was again, Wolfe, Trevalian and myself all alone with Lord Dunning, although this time, I was pretty sure that we would have the last word.

I looked around the bloated, burst carcass of Judy's father, the sickly-sweet smell of death already starting to fill the air. It had been a good shot, for that was what had accelerated Dunning's departure from this life, ahead of cholesterol.

Wolfe sat down in the corner of the room, a wrinkled, dirty white handkerchief whipped out of his dinner jacket breast pocket, was now being used to dab repeatedly at his sweating brow.

'You two carry on,' he panted, 'I'll make notes.'

The round had entered the deceased's back mid-point of the shoulder blades, the exit point being right through his lower abdomen. This was fairly easy to deduce, as the desk behind which Lord Dunning was now lolling, was missing, splintered and ruptured beneath the gore.

The high backed leather seat which was supporting the dead mans frame, revealed a neat single hole high in its centre which I could see clearly would match the entry point of the round in the dead man's back.

So Dunning had been sat back in his chair when the shot struck him from behind.

As I looked at the exit wound, I noticed a black powdery residue on his jacket, a mark I was sure was not there previously when we were all in the dining room together. Nervously, I reached out and pushed my fingers into the deep folds of fat in the dead man's neck, seeking out the carotid pulse.

It seemed the right thing to do.

He was definitely dead.

'Do you agree?' asked Trevalian, his tone told me he resented my double check, openly doubting his professional assessment.

I quickly withdrew my hand. 'Sorry, you're the expert.' I put both hands in the air in mock surrender.

I looked back through the shattered windowpane. The clouds had decided once more to unleash another downpour upon us; eerily it seemed to give the appearance that the island was in mourning.

I pulled down one of the finely manufactured, heavy, thick designer labelled curtains and draped it gently over the late Lord, in death, all hatred for this man was beginning to wane. With Trevalian's help, I covered the body.

No person deserved a violent death like this, regardless of what kind of a bastard they had been in life.

Again the sky was sliced in two by a bolt of lightning racing across the sky, a roar of thunder following a second behind it.

The sound of a stormy sea assailing the cliffs of the island in the near distance, whoever had fired the fatal round that had ended the life of this most hated man, was trapped on the island with us, he or she had killed once, the question was, would they kill again?

I could tell it was going to be a long, hard night; few if any of us would sleep tonight.

'This will make a great story,' mumbled Wolfe, smiling happily. 'Definitely front page.'

Trevalian, turning his back on the journalist in disgust at his ghoulish joy, called out to me, 'Cole, until the police arrive, I'm going to do a few quick checks on the body.'

Nodding, in deep thought, I went out into the hall, closing the door securely behind me.

Donald had been asked to get Mary to phone the police. I went to the telephone table in the hallway, near the front door, just in case, the thought *who can you trust*? niggling at the back of my mind.

Would Mary make the call?

Was Trevalian hiding something? I did not know. Just in case, I decided two calls were better than none.

I picked up the receiver and… Nothing, the line was dead.

The killer, whoever he or she was, had us trapped here on the island, in the house; we were cut off from any help. Ever seen the old black and white movie *And Then There Were None*? I have, several times. I was getting a little worried.

I decided that, for the time being, no one else needed to know about the phones not working, just in case it upset them or they panicked.

I replaced the dead receiver and went across to the dining room, pushing the door open. Donald was just inside, serving copious amounts of brandy to everyone who was sitting dejectedly in the many high backed seats around the dining table.

As I entered, all eyes in the room fell upon me, and Donald, noticing this, made his way across to me.

'Still want me to keep them out?' he whispered.

'May as well,' I shrugged, 'Wolfe and Trevalian are in there now, besides Lord Dunning won't want any more visitors for a while.'

The image of the shredded remains of the deceased Lord swam back into my mind's eye and I shuddered involuntarily. This did not go unnoticed by Donald who was busy pouring a heavy, decorative, lead crystal decanter of brandy into an empty glass, on the other end of it was Judy.

The glazed look in her eyes told me she had offered up the empty glass many times in the last few minutes.

I remember her telling me when we first met, that she was a social drinker, I could see now she was as sociable as a newt.

'Problem?' asked Donald quietly.

'No, of course not.' But something had just registered in the back of my mind.

An inconsistency, something which didn't add up, it was like an itch that at this moment I couldn't scratch; but I knew the answer to how to stop this itching lay in the room with the dead man. 'You, stay here with everyone else, I need to check something.'

I left the dining room again and pulled the door closed behind me. I crossed the marble hallway and, taking a deep breath, pushed open the study door and entered.

Trevalian and Wolfe were discussing the finer points of medical ethics as I entered. Both doctor and journalist instantly ceased their debate as I entered the room.

'Everything all right?' asked Wolfe, still sitting sweating in the old leather chair, well away from the body.

'Just need to check something,' I replied absently, lost in thought.

The broken windowpane, high in the window frame was letting just enough fresh sea air through to reduce the smell of death and leaking bodily gases from the ruptured husk of the body to a tolerable level.

A little observing, without of course disturbing the crime scene, revealed several interesting points which, on my first nervous examination I had overlooked.

Gingerly, I lifted up the now stained curtain from the body and, thanking the university gymnasium, managed to move Lord Dunning back against the shattered chair back. His vast stomach and chest clawed out from within by the force of the spinning lead projectile.

The deep crimson black stain already spread to its fullest as the wounds in the front and back of the body continued to bleed. In retrospect, his body wasn't actually bleeding, just leaking badly.

What had struck me earlier in the dining room when I mentally revisited the scene, was the realisation that there were of course two wounds, not just the wounds to the front and back of the body, but the black powdery residue on the front of the jacket, suggesting loudly that they were in fact powder burns, consistent with a close quarter assault from the front.

Carefully, I pulled the jacket back, there, hidden in the pooling blood, in the corpse's chest, was a hole. Consistent with small arms weaponry. I estimated probably a 9mm or a .45 calibre pistol.

'Michael, look at this.'

Trevalian quickly joined me. Wolfe, due to his obvious discomfort with death, remained well to the rear although I noticed he did shift himself to lean closer to us, to be a not so covert eavesdropper on our conversation.

Around the obvious bullet wound, several small black pepper marks tattooed the dead mans flesh across his ample punctured torso.

'Powder burns,' stated Trevalian nodding to himself. 'Small calibre firearm discharge about six to eight inches distant,' he concluded.

'Yes, that's what I thought,' I concurred.

'Saw it all the time in Columbia, arguments between the drug cartels.'

Wolfe suddenly discovered some hitherto unknown inner resolve and overcame his revulsion.

'He was shot twice?' Obvious excitement in his voice.

Trevalian eyed him coldly before replying slowly, 'Looks that way.'

'Great. This just keeps getting better and better.' Wolfe rubbed his hands together briskly. 'So, who did it?' His eyes jumped from me to Trevalian and back to me again.

I glanced quickly at Trevalian, catching his quizzing gaze as I replied, unconvincingly, 'I don't know.'

A quick scan around the room, under the desk, under the chairs, tables and the edges of the room proved that no cartridge had been ejected. I concluded that the tool used to complete this task must have been either a revolver or the killer was meticulously tidy.

But it still did not add up. The way the chest and abdomen had been torn out negated the theory of a one-man attack. The projectile that had ripped through the lord's back was obviously a high-powered weapon.

The round had smashed through the French windows, the solid oak chair back, Lord Dunning himself and probably to his great surprise, disappeared through the oak study desk and, following its trajectory, was probably lodged somewhere in the wine cellar in the basement.

I stepped around the chair and pushed open the unlocked French doors, shards of glass fell awkwardly out of the frame, smashing on to the hard stone balcony floor outside.

'So much for protecting the murder scene,' sighed Trevalian, following me out on to the balcony, the garden lights were already on due to the darkness.

It was ample light to search quickly for what I was looking for.

The rain, still falling, failed to reach me, limited, but not total protection from the elements offered by the narrow veranda of the bedrooms above. I quickly examined the tattered remains of the French windows for powder marks or spent cases on the balcony. I was so deep in concentration and examination of the area, that I failed to realise how soaked I was getting, until I returned to the study, water pooling around my sodden black dinner suit trousers.

Trevalian following me back inside, 'Find anything?'

I shook my head, 'No.'

I knew that I needed to talk to Lady Dunning. Something was missing.

'Can you and Tim stay here?' I continued, thoughts racing through my mind.

As Tim Wolfe began to object, obviously fearing he was going to lose another angle for his paper, Trevalian grabbed him, holding him firmly in situ.

'Yes, no problem. We'll stay, just in case they come back.'

Wolfe brightened, 'You think they might?'

'You never *know*,' whispered the doctor smiling.

On re-entering the dining room, I was again aware of every eye suspiciously following my every move as I crossed the room.

I also noted the obvious absence of the major and Miss Frobisher.

Lady Forsythe was sitting in the corner of the room, quietly downing the brandy so thoughtfully supplied by Donald. She was visibly shaking.

Lady Dunning was sobbing sorrowfully into Judy's shoulder as mother and daughter attempted to console each other for their mutual loss.

Donald maintained a steady supply of alcohol, as soon as someone appeared to be coming to the alcohol smeared bottom of their tumbler, he was on hand with the decanter, like a juggler spinning plates, he maintained the alcoholic haze.

It seemed like a good solution to everyone's immediate problems.

I noticed Donald secretly partaking of the odd belt himself, for medicinal purposes of course.

Lady Dunning obviously had other things on her mind.

'Excuse me, where are the major and Miss Frobisher?'

My voice must have cut through the drunken veil like a knife, the stony, stunned silence of the room echoing to my half-shouted request.

The slurred voice of Lady Forsythe called back, 'My husband has gone upstairs to freshen up.' Three parts cut and gaining ground on unconsciousness rapidly. Through the slur of her alcohol-tainted announcement, my trained ear was able to filter out the odd repeated and mumbled word so that I could understand.

I have noticed over the years that drunks seem to be able to speak their own alien language, only understood by those living in the same alcoholic haze. With years of practise, I had been able to train myself to understand this language. My studies in practical alcohol abuse 101 at university were beginning to pay off.

Judy mumbled something about Miss Frobisher; Jayne, was in the kitchen with Mary, the reason for this she did not provide.

I made my way carefully across the dining room to Lady Dunning, and, using the tone of voice I usually reserved for my more attractive female students, who needed some extra encouragement to provide their papers on time, I asked, quietly and with feeling, 'I know it's difficult, but can you remember what actually happened in there?'

My syrupy smooth velvet tones always made me want to throw up, but my track record remained constant, it worked as it always did.

The widow Dunning stopped blubbering and, wiping her tearful eyes; 'I saw a man, he was wearing black or dark clothing with something over his face and head,' she mumbled.

'Where? Where did you see him?' I reached out and gently took hold of her hand, squeezing it reassuringly.

'He... He was on the balcony, he was just suddenly there, no warning, no nothing.'

'What was he doing?'

'He seemed to have a gun, a long one, he had to use both hands to hold it.' She stopped and became withdrawn, several seconds passed without a word being said.

'Go on, you're doing very well.' I tried to encourage her to continue with her remembrance of the events leading to her husbands demise.

'He... He just aimed and fired through the French windows, the gun looked like the one that was stolen.'

'Did you recognise the man? Did he say or do anything famil-iar?'

She shook her head. 'I presume it was the same man that the major saw and chased off earlier. He didn't say anything and I don't know who it could have been.'

'That's great,' I replied encouragingly. 'What happened next?'

'After shooting Martin, the man just jumped over the balus-trade of the balcony and then sprinted off across the lawn towards the old disused jetty.'

'Did you see anyone else?' I asked.

Even in her slightly drunken state, Judy must have noticed the change in the tone of my voice because she looked up and eyed me curiously.

'No.' The sobbing returned and her body began to shake with the uncontrolled grief.

'I know it's difficult, we're nearly there,' I started, soothing tones again. I stroked her hand reassuringly, 'Can you just give me a little more?'

She nodded that she could, or at least that she would try. Sev-eral deep breaths later, she seemed to regain some semblance of control.

'Can you tell me, how many times did this man shoot?'

'Twice. Once, I can't remember clearly.' She had gone, the sobbing returning with a vengeance, her slim frame shaking violently, crying hysterically once more, I knew there was nothing more I was going to get from her tonight.

'Who would want to see my Daddy dead?' asked Judy, pouting and trying to be brave for her mother's sake, her stiff upper lip quivering slightly.

In reply, I felt like handing her the telephone directory and telling her to take her pick.

But deep down, I knew that she didn't need to hear that.

'I don't know, Judy, I really don't.'

'Cole, find the person who did this, please,' she begged.

I shook my head slowly. I felt that there was little more that I could do.

'You've called the police?' she whispered, looking away at her hands, already trying to tie knots in the flowing skirts of her beautiful evening dress.

'Yes,' I lied, turning away from her lest she catch the deceit in my eyes, 'they'll be here tomorrow.'

She looked me full in the face, her hands now grasping mine.

'So, until then, do something, anything to find my father's killer.'

'Judy, I wish I could, but the police...'

'Won't be here until tomorrow,' she interrupted. 'If you love me, you'll do this, just until the police arrive and take over.'

'But...'

'Cole, I need to know someone is doing something. I know you can do it.'

I was about to point out the futility of what she was demanding, instead, on seeing the resolve set in her almond shaped eyes, I satisfied myself with looking around the room at all the persons still present.

Each one, including myself had a motive, but we all had a near perfect alibi, we were each other's.

The face of this unknown assassin escaped me. 'All right.'

Away in the distance, the church bell solemnly tolled a mournful nine times, adding an unwanted depth to the sorrow displayed by Judy and her mother.

'Have you called the police yet?' asked Lady Barton from her place at the table, gently sipping a delicate sherry.

'Yes, of course,' I lied. I noticed out of the corner of my eye Donald stealing a disbelieving and suspicious look in my direction.

'Good! How long before they arrive and take charge?' came the question from behind me. It was the major.

I turned to see the military man standing in the doorway, his jet-black hair wet from the shower.

'Sometime tomorrow morning.' I tried my poker face again and played for a bluff.

I could tell Judy knew me far too well. She stared open-mouthed at me. The expression on her face, eyes wide open, she knew I had lied to her.

'The weather,' I offered as an explanation to the unasked

question.

'Cole!' she snapped. 'What are you...?'

'Judy!' I snarled back. 'Shut up and look after your mother!'

I know it was a harsh thing to say, but I had to do it. The other occupants of the room looked at me with distaste, scorn and disgust in their eyes.

Later, I hoped Judy would forgive me.

For now, she burst into unyielding tears, sobbing hysterically with her mother, like a mourning tag team.

'Donald,' I called beckoning him to come to me, 'can you come with me, please?' Donald's' eyes narrowed and he nodded slowly and suspiciously.

'Major, please stay in this room and look after the ladies.'

The look on his face was pure disgust and obstinately he folded his arms in defiance, 'I most certainly will not!' He planted his feet firmly, shoulder width apart, his patent leather clad feet embedded in the thick dining room carpet. The stance was one of open defiance, I guessed he was trying to stamp his authority on the developing situation as he continued, yelling, 'Who the devil put you in charge! I'm an officer in Her Majesty's Armed Forces I'll have you know, I'm used to *giving* orders not *taking* them, and I refuse point blank to take orders from a civilian of your standing!'

'Really?' I asked sarcastically.

I looked across at John Simmons. He was sitting quietly hugging his sobbing wife. I guessed that she wasn't upset about Dunning's demise, but more likely what it signified for her and her husband's crusade for justice.

'I'm the senior ranking officer here, I should be in charge until the authorities arrive,' continued the major on his original tack, his tone challenging me to disagree with him.

I had had as much of this man as I could stomach, with anger in my voice, I turned to him and said simply, 'Major, pull rank on this!' I delivered a quick one fingered gesture to summarise my feelings so that he was left in no uncertainty as to what high esteem I held him in. I turned to John Simmons as I heard the now disillusioned major mumble in self-pity, 'But I'm a major.' All the fight, anger and resolve were quickly dissipating.

'Oh Forsythe! For heaven's sake, for once in your life shut up and listen to what someone else has to say!' Lady Barton's voice was quite insistent.

Surprisingly, the major instantly capitulated.

Lady Barton looked over to me, 'You just need to know how to handle some little boys. He hasn't changed any. Was the same bombastic little oik when he worked for my late husband.' She smiled at the obvious discomfort the major was now bathed in as he sat himself-dejectedly in a nearby leather chair.

'Oh, your husband was in the army then?' I asked.

'Well, yes he was, at one stage. But Forsythe here was not in the army at the same time. He only became an officer after marrying Lady Charlton as she was then.'

'Oh really.' I smiled at the major in acknowledgement of his position as another embarrassing skeleton was dragged from the cupboard of his past.

'Yes, he needed someone to get his military career back on track, always was a bit of a mummy's boy.'

Still grinning, I turned to the major who was looking indignantly at Lady Barton, obviously wishing either she would die or the ground would open up and swallow him. I was just about to comment on this with a suitably derived and properly weighted insult, when Lady Dunning let out an elongated squeal, which instantly drew everyone's attention.

I looked over to her, knowing full well that my eardrums would never survive another tearful and unrelenting dirge. For the sake of my hearing and my sanity, I made my excuses and left the room.

I pulled the dining room door closed behind me.

Donald was waiting in the hallway. Together we returned to the study.

'How long has Mary known Miss Frobisher?' I asked, trying to break the brooding, suspicion filled silence that now occupied the void between us.

'I don't know,' he mumbled in reply. I was aware of his eyes never leaving me.

It was as if the trust and understanding that had developed earlier between us had been completely shattered and now an air of distrust and suspicion clung to our every movement. It seemed like an eternity as we crossed the huge hall, the awkward silence straining to near breaking point. Eventually we entered the study.

Wolfe and Trevalian were waiting for us within.

'What on earth was that scream?' asked Wolfe nervously.

'Lady Dunning,' I replied simply. Turning to Trevalian, 'Judy's asked me to find the killer.'

'Good luck,' he shrugged. 'Where do you intend starting, Sherlock?'

'May as well be here.'

I began to make a detailed inspection of the highly polished oak panels and velvet-like wallpaper.

'So what are we actually looking for?' Wolfe finally asked as I cautiously checked the walls around the dead man's study. I noticed Donald's eyes never leaving my back.

'Don't know,' I replied honestly, deep in concentration. 'I'll let you know when I find it.' I continued picking my way around the room, constantly aware of the piercing eyes of the butler.

The clock tower chimed out the hour of ten before any of us spoke again.

'So, what do you want me to do?' Donald's tone hadn't changed – his voice was still heavy with suspicion and accusation.

'Well,' I began, trying to figure how best to present my suspicion, 'I believe that one of the party guests, invited by Lady Dunning has used the opportunity to either kill Lord Dunning, or arranged for someone else to carry out the deed. Either way, someone in the dining room is linked directly to this murder.'

I attempted to present it matter-of-factly. I was sure that even one of my first year students would have already come to that same determination fairly quickly, I tried to stress the need never to assume anything, but there could be no other explanation at this time.

But who?

'Really?' Wolfe asked, his voice excited at the possibility of more scandal.

'Who do you suspect?' asked Donald, he was hooked, his voice now betraying some of its previous warmth toward me.

'Everyone,' I replied, shrugging. 'I need you to do something for me.'

Wolfe interrupted, 'Go ahead, I'm your man. What do you need doing?' The excitement was now manifest. If he got any more interested or excited, he'd be jumping and clapping. I ignored him.

'Donald, I need you to check upstairs, check the guests' rooms.'

'What for?' he asked.

'Primarily, letters, invitations, shoes, anything that appears out of place or wrong.'

'Shoes?' he snapped, a barely restrained laugh mixed with the incredulous, curious and questioning look that he shot me.

'Yes,' I confirmed. 'Shoes.'

Trevalian and Wolfe exchanged curiosity piqued glances at each other as Donald stifling his laughter asked, 'Why?' when he saw that I was serious.

'It may be nothing,' I replied, 'but I have a hunch, and I always follow my hunches, so let's check that out too.'

'Okay.'

Donald turned and disappeared through the study doorway, pulling the door closed behind him.

Trevalian shifted his gaze to me as he repeated Donald's question, 'Shoes?'

'Yes, I'll tell you all about it later, in the meantime, I need you and Tim to go back to the dining room.'

'And do what?' asked Wolfe, looking from the doctor to myself and back again.

'See if you can find anything there that may shed some light on all this.'

Trevalian nodded and crossed the room to the door, his massive frame towering above the overweight journalist who was still watching us both keenly.

'And look for what, exactly?' Wolfe stared at me now, his deep-set eyes, for once still, locked my gaze on his.

'I don't know,' with a great effort of will, I broke his almost hypnotic piercing stare, 'you're the investigative journalist. Go investigate.'

'Hell,' he scoffed, tucking his sodden handkerchief back into his breast pocket. 'I usually get to make stuff up to fit the facts.'

'I don't doubt it for a second,' sighed Trevalian, herding the journalist, shuffling out of the study. The door eased closed behind them and instantly the stench of death assailed my nostrils as I was left alone with the corpse.

I spent the next ten minutes staring in silent confusion at the remnants of the shattered French windows. It was then that a small hole in the right-hand, vertical stone lintel caught my eye.

I considered the possibility that the unknown masked gunman had probably discharged his weapon by accident, and fired a subsequent shot through the lintel after his first shot had destroyed the French windows.

Another streak of lightning flashed across the dark cloth of the night, slicing the heavens in two with its brilliant silvery arc.

There, silhouetted beautifully in that moment of intense white silvery hot light, was the clock tower, situated precisely on the horizon at the end of the croquet lawn, dominating the skyline.

It summed up Lord Dunning perfectly, most people had a wristwatch but Lord Dunning had been able to just turn around and look up at the clock tower and see…

The clock tower! The idea hit me like a truck.

The clock tower would have been a perfect elevated observation point for a second gunman. And a good hideout. I walked out on to the balcony, through the shattered window, the clock face captured in my field of vision.

Yes, it felt right, I could feel the hypothetical cross hairs of the sniper's sights creeping across my chest, as I stood and watched for any movement that would betray the firing position.

I looked back at the shattered chair back, the angle matched, the shot must have come from the clock tower, there could be no mistake.

It was an afterthought really. I noticed again that the rain had not eased up. Leaning heavily on the balustrade, I looked down the ten feet or so to the soft, muddy, picture perfect grassed lawn below.

I wondered where the masked murderer had landed in his flight to escape his sole surviving witness. Jumping from this height, he must have made a fairly impressive impact on the soft grass.

I looked around my feet on the balcony floor, there, near the shattered door, I saw a broken wooden batten about four inches long, one inch wide, its edges jagged and snapped.

Casually I tossed the wooden debris on to the lawn. With an audible squelch, the batten embedded itself easily in the soft grass for about a quarter of its length.

I went back into the study, only now realising how cold it was.

I needed a clean shirt, shoes and to get out of the penguin suit which was now sodden and ruined with rain water, blood and other dead Dunning residue.

I made my way through the study, across the hall and up the stairs to my room. As I made my way up the stairs towards my landing, I encountered a perplexed looking Donald coming the other way.

'Well?' I asked as we met on the stairway.

'Nothing,' he shrugged.

'What do you mean nothing?' I asked, dripping uncontrollably on to the marble steps.

'Well, everyone has invitations, as you'd expect, all signed by Lady Dunning herself. I recognised the signature.'

'And?' I prompted again.

'And nothing, that's it.'

Scuppered.

'Oh well,' I sighed, 'just a hunch anyway as I said, at least we've exhausted that line of enquiry. Can you go back to the dining room for me. Wait for me there with Doctor Trevalian and Mr Wolfe, I'll be down in a few minutes, okay?' Donald nodded and made his way downstairs.

I reached my own room and quickly changed out of the penguin suit and frilly white shirt, into jeans, sweat top and my favourite cross trainers. I pulled my leather jacket out of the wardrobe and carried it with me, just in case a trip outside was called for.

Refreshed and comfortable at last.

I made my way back to the dining room where the guests were, hopefully, still waiting, drowning themselves in brandy and sherry.

I had reached the first landing – this was the floor where I knew all the other dinner guests had been lodged, where Donald had been so monumentally unsuccessful.

I decided to eliminate the hunch totally. I needed to check things for myself. I made my way cautiously down the corridor into the guests' quarters, flitting from shadow to shadow, doing my best not to be seen.

Why? Well, I don't really know, but they do it in all the films, and besides, it felt right.

If I could get in and out of the rooms without being seen, it would mean less explaining at the end of the day.

I could hear my father in the back of my mind remonstrating and lecturing me on the Police and Criminal Evidence Act, illegal searches and any evidence gained during an illegal search would be inadmissible. But in my mind, it only affected law enforcement officers. After all, I was just being nosy.

Remembering that Stephen Carpenter had retired early, I knocked his door to obtain his co-operation and assistance, after all, he was a legal eagle and likely to sue my ass right out of university if I upset him by invading his privacy.

Knocking loudly several times achieved nothing.

I tried the door experimentally. It was securely locked. Cautiously, I peered through the keyhole, only to find that the key was in the lock on the inside of the room.

A few more heavy knocks and my shouting for him to open the door only proved that whatever he had taken to numb the pain, was numbing his hearing too. I resolved to take the matter up with him at breakfast.

Jayne Frobisher's room was the first I managed to gain entry to, the door on this occasion, was unlocked. I quickly searched the wardrobe and drawers.

Jayne Frobisher had a very interesting wardrobe it had to be said, her lingerie was exciting and sexy, I made a mental note to discuss some of the items with Judy later.

Her suitcase was lying open on the top of her bed, inside I found a neatly folded painting, it was childlike and bright, a name written in childish scrawl revealed the budding artist to be Martyn

Frobisher aged four.

I replaced it back in the suitcase carefully, as I did so, I noticed a picture frame tucked neatly into a pile of towels, obviously Jayne Frobisher had never been to Lady Dunning's home before, at least, I thought, not while Lady Dunning had been here.

It was obvious that Jayne Frobisher was used to living out of suitcases.

I gingerly pulled the ornamental, metal-framed picture free. Looking at it, I recognised a slightly younger Jayne with a babe in arms, for all the world she looked happy and contented with her lot.

Remembering that Judy had the infuriating habit of writing a synopsis of the event captured on film, on the reverse of every holiday snap we had ever taken, I found myself wondering if this was a general female trait.

Carefully, I removed the plate at the rear of the polished, ornate frame. A small, carefully folded note floated freely from the back of the picture, floating gently down on to the counter-pane of the bed.

Curiously, I picked it up and gently unfolded it. It read:

My dearest Jayne, I cannot accept this gift, look after my son, I will find a way to ensure he has everything he needs, please do not think ill of me, Helen would never understand.

I refolded the note and turned my attention back to the picture of the smiling young woman with the babe in arms. There it was, a simple dedication, *With love from Jayne and Martyn, we will always love you, your distant but caring other family*. The picture was dated just four years ago.

I secured the note back in the rear of the frame and secreted the picture back in the case.

Some things, I thought, are better left unknown.

The next bedroom I found myself in was the quiet Mr Stanford's. The room was just like him, nothing more interesting that an executive perpetual motion toy. The suitcases were locked and nothing more than the toy and toiletries had been unpacked from the small overnight bag in the bathroom.

Drake, the Londoner was in the next room. He had already laid his room out. Under his bed I found an unlocked black leather executive briefcase, inside it, under a pile of other papers and files was a manila envelope file, marked simply DUNNING.

The envelope was unsealed and it was a simple matter to open it and check the contents. Inside the envelope, I found it contained photographs, newspaper clippings and letters from one JS.

The clippings were all regarding Lord Dunning's past close encounters of the Miss Frobisher kind, his mistress and photographs of a pretty young teenage girl, on the back of the picture the name *Lucy* had been written in red ink, I wondered if this could be a picture of Lucy Simmons, before her addiction and death. If it was, I wondered, what is it doing here?

A letter in the envelope was on letter headed paper from the desk of Lord Martin Dunning MP. It was addressed to Drake and pointed out that he would never submit to blackmail and refused to go through with some financial arrangement, which had obviously been agreed to earlier between the two parties.

The letter from the mysterious JS was requesting an update on progress so far.

On checking the corresponding envelopes, I discovered they were all addressed to a confidential contact *make a date* newspaper box number at a local newspaper. I replaced the documents into the envelope, replaced the envelope into the briefcase and secured it again, returning it to its hiding place.

I carefully removed all evidence of my visit and left the room.

Carefully I made my way down the dimly lit landing to another of the guest's bedrooms. The door, as the previous ones, was unlocked.

On entering, I discovered that the room had been allocated to John and Sylvia. It was as I had expected. Comfortable and cosy, nothing untoward or out of place.

Unsurprisingly normal.

The next room was that of Lady Barton. It too was comfortable, her invitation had pride of place between a recent photograph of a rather pampered poodle I took to be the delightful and distracting Bopsey, whom she had spoken of earlier in the evening and a yellowed and faded old photograph of a young man.

Carefully, I picked up the yellowed photo in its heavy and ornate gold frame, this captured memory that Lady Barton held in such reverence was in remarkable condition.

It clearly showed a man, handsome and proud in his early twenties standing stiffly in front of a shop, the placard above the old shop front reading BARTON'S WATCH AND CLOCK REPAIRS TO KING AND COUNTRY – certainly a name to boast about.

I remembered my father telling me the story of the little clock mender. Until recently I had thought the story was a modern-day fairy tale, teaching me that anything was possible, whatever the odds.

I could clearly see that Mr Barton, as he was then, was certainly no fairy tale, just a hard working, ordinary man with a special gift for clockwork engineering.

Now, this and his widow had my admiration for the struggle they had both endured.

I placed the picture frame gently back on the mantelpiece in the bedroom and continued my search for something, anything which would connect one of the guests to the untimely demise of Lord Dunning.

In the bedside drawer, I found several letters from Lady Helen Dunning to Lady Emily Barton.

Reading between the lines, Lady Dunning was announcing to the world, she was sick and fed up of being the unpopular wife of the most despised lord in the country, she wanted to do something about it and escape the unhappy marriage she felt trapped in and to put down, once and for all, the mask of subservience she wore for the eyes of the ever critical world press.

I thought Wolfe would love to get his hands on these.

The letters went on to reveal that she, Lady Dunning had indeed met another man, someone who made her feel young and alive, someone who loved her for who she was not what she was.

This man had rekindled the warmth of love in her heart and now she had filed for divorce, the first step in escaping the clutches of the evil lord's domain.

Lord Dunning was of course contesting the divorce and resisting the legal procedures because of the huge scandal it would cause.

He had, she said, instructed his solicitors to rewrite his will and they were under instructions not to reveal its contents to her.

Patrick Holliday, one of the partners, and a close personal friend of Lady Dunning, had told her simply that he was powerless to indulge her whilst Stephen Carpenter, one of the other partners was acting on behalf of Lord Dunning.

Lady Dunning was upset and could see no way out to reach her happiness. Lady Barton, in her replies, referred to in the letters, was offering support and understanding, but little else. I replaced the letters and made good my escape.

Major and Lady Forsythe's room was uninteresting too. He seemed to live and breathe the doctrines of the military, both his and his wife's drawers laid out neatly in regimental orderliness. I felt like checking the neat piles with a ruler or set square, but could see no point, as they were obviously perfect.

On opening the large walk-in closet, which had been a feature of the other rooms, I saw neatly, displayed, three hanging shoe racks, one for him, two for her. His shoes were each in neatly press-stud fastened opaque pouches, each clearly labelled Monday through to Sunday. I wondered if hers were labelled nine to ten, ten to noon. But no, they were just kept wrapped in tissue paper, fresh and clean.

This to me was the height of the rich life. I had three pairs of shoes and one pair of trainers which I wore for everything, not designer labelled like these shoes, mine were Hush Puppies and New Balance not Gucci and Paco Rabanne. The clothing hung here continued in the same vein, everything designer labelled.

A twinge of jealousy?

Certainly not, the thought, *Bugger all in the fridge but three dozen £200 shirts in the wardrobe, discarded after being worn once* flashed across my mind, my sister had gone through a similar stage years ago, she now used her money more productively, by, it has to be said, not giving any to me.

A flash of lightning again raced across the heavens, cutting the night sky in half. From here, I wondered which part of the garden I could see. I walked over to the closed window.

As I did so, I noticed the lush deep carpet beneath the window squelch audibly under foot, water oozing over the top of my training shoe.

Typical, I thought, Lady Forsythe had probably aired the room when she arrived, something both Judy and my mother had always done whenever we'd gone anywhere overnight, whether or not the room needed it.

Either Lady Dunning or Mary would be livid when they found out. The carpet was going to stink like hell.

I looked out of the window into the garden, as I did so, the first thing that caught my eye were two dirty rectangular marks about fourteen inches apart on the neat, white painted ledge outside the window.

A thought occurred to me, and I went back to the walk-in wardrobe. I checked 'his' hanging shoe rack again, the shoes were all Gucci, but none were missing.

I opened the pouch marked Wednesday and removed the pair of highly polished black Gucci shoes from the pouch. I noted that the right shoe had a small piece of clean white paper stuck to the sole, strangely, none of the major's other shoes were so adorned, this pair did not appear to have been worn yet.

I looked back into the pouch, there, trapped at the bottom of the otherwise empty pouch was a piece of neat, clean tissue paper, none of the other shoe envelopes were equipped in this way, in my mind, my suspicion was confirmed.

I tided the room, something Judy told me frequently, I never did at home. By the time I was finished, all traces of my visit had been removed.

I hoped.

Although Judy could always tell what I had cleaned up and what I hadn't, I hoped that the major and his wife were not so observant.

Trevalian and Wolfe's doors were both locked and I decide to take the matter up with them both later.

I made my way back upstairs, stopping briefly in my appointed room to dig out my trusty, reliable black metal Maglite torch. For what I had in mind, I knew that I would need it.

I met Donald at the door to the dining room, the strain of being alone with this menagerie of whinging and bickering socialites was beginning to tell on even his professionally maintained countenance.

I beckoned him to one side; he joined me in the hallway, closing the dining room door behind him.

'Everything all right?' I asked, dreading an answer.

'Thank God you're back. I don't know how much more I can take of this,' he sighed.

'You're doing fine,' I reassured him patronisingly. 'Didn't they teach you how to cope with situations like this back in butler school?' I asked.

Donald looked at me, his blank expression conveying more than most words.

'No,' he stated emphatically. 'I was ill the day they taught us how to deal with your employer being brutally murdered, and how to cope with distressed party guests who may also be psychopathic killers. I must take that up with them – perhaps I can do make-up tests.' His expression did not falter, the tone in his voice remaining disturbingly calm and rational.

'Tell Doctor Trevalian and Wolfe that I'm going outside, be sure not to tell anyone else.'

'Why?'

'Because… Look, do you have a watch?' I asked, trying to change the focus of our conversation.

He nodded the fact that he had.

'Good, I need you to time me. Note the time I leave the hall and the time I return.'

'Why?'

'I just want to check out a theory I'm working on,' I explained. 'Can you do that?'

Again he nodded that he could. 'Sure.' He looked at his watch and then continued, 'Look, it's late, some of the ladies would like to retire.'

'I thought at their age, most of them already had.'

'No, they want to go to bed,' he restated. 'Is it all right?' Again the tone of his voice told me that it was a mute point, they would be going up to their rooms whether or not I thought it safe and appropriate.

I looked at my watch. It was now near midnight. It had been a long and tiring day, dead tiring for some.

'Yes, of course,' I agreed. I turned and went back to the study.

I prepared myself. Pulling my torch from my pocket, I switched it on and focused the beam into an intense, bright narrow beam of light.

I checked my wristwatch, the second hand on Mickey's face was sweeping slowly through its cycle, and, as it sliced past twelve, I took several deep breaths and then, I was away at a full sprint, my arms and legs pumping furiously as I sped out of the French doors, down the balcony steps, taking them three or four at a time, across the soft and boggy croquet lawn, through the rose garden and on to the uneven path, the lights from the house lit my way most of the way across the lawn, but in the shade of the rose garden, darkness reigned supreme.

The moon, although not full was casting a bright and eerie light down around me, the clouds which were still overhead and leaking profusely occasionally blocking the lunar light.

My Maglite did the rest.

The uneven path led, I knew from my travels earlier in the day, straight to the church and then beyond it, down to the disused cove and its broken wooden jetty.

At full sprint, I reached the large ornate stone arch of the church entrance, I was completely knackered, out of breath and wheezing heavily, the rain and my exertions adding together to ensure that I was as wet and uncomfortable as it was possible to be.

I again checked my wristwatch. The full sprint run to the church had taken me three minutes. I noticed that the old wooden and iron banded church doors were unlocked.

The iron bound keyhole showing signs of recent use, a quick scan with my trusty torch showed several sets of muddy foot-prints leading both into and out of the church, but the weather had easily concealed any evidence which may have been obtained.

I knew my father and his colleagues had equipment and the technology to remedy this, but here and now, I only had my eyes. If there was something inside the church, I decided that I could cover and preserve any footprint evidence that could be used to track Dunning's murderer.

The door opened easily and I slid in, quietly; trying to ensure that anyone inside would be unaware of my presence, retaining the all-important element of surprise for myself. I closed the large doors behind me. The hinges and old wood moaning in protest as the door closed fully; the empty thud of the old wood resounding around the empty old church.

I used my torch to quickly scan the floor before me, again it was no more than cold stone, clean and dry, someone had already been here and removed any incriminating footprints. Several candles had been lit here recently. I switched off the torch and quickly peered through the dim flickering candlelight for any person who may have been alerted by my arrival.

It was quite disturbing.

The saints and angels, embedded in their stained glass and lead prisons stared down at me, almost it seemed in anticipation, of what? I did not know.

The church was quiet, every movement seeming to echo off the ancient freezing stone.

'Quiet as the grave,' I mumbled under my breath and immediately wished I hadn't, the hairs on the back of my neck rising. The feeling of being watched by some unseen supernatural force was not far from my thoughts.

The old stone seemed to draw the heat from my body as I wandered carefully and slowly through the wooden and stone pews, columns and marble statues.

After my exertion from the running, I was now chilling rapidly and several shivers ran up and down my spine. Someone obviously tended this place with loving care.

I checked the sconces in the walls as I carefully and quietly edged my way around the chapel. The candles were fresh I noticed, recently lit, I saw that the molten tallow which dripped down each candle and into the basin of the sconces was consistent, and very little wax had so far rolled down the body of the candles.

Then it hit me.

Literally.

What it was exactly I couldn't tell. Heavy and blunt would

have been my description to anyone asking me about it later. All I knew at that precise moment was that it hurt like hell and the whole dimly lit world around me blinked out into complete and unforgiving darkness.

I do not recall hitting the floor.

From somewhere far away, I heard a faint voice calling me in the dark.

'Mr Meredith? Mr Meredith, can you hear me? Are you all right?' The voice was dull and muffled, it sounded like the owner was eating a pullover or some other woollen or fabric item.

From somewhere off in the distance, I heard low moaning. It took several seconds to realise that these moans were coming from my own throat.

In sympathy to the resonance, my head was pounding, pain was trying to force a way through the agony I was feeling. I was dimly aware of something cold and liquid dripping past my right eye, down to my ear and after that, well, I didn't much care where it went after that, I was just glad that cold meant that it probably wasn't blood.

My eyes were reluctant to open, but carefully I managed this great feat.

First the left and then the right.

I knew that something was wrong when I saw half a dozen faces, all with similar features swimming ethereally above me, shimmering and swirling in the flickering half-light of the candles. Slowly, the floating disembodied faces merged briefly into one, then once more they span off at tangents, a nauseous feeling rising in the pit of my stomach, burning the back of my dry throat.

Blinking hard, it took several seconds before my blurred vision was able to focus and the faces finally melded into one and stayed that way.

'I'm sorry Mr Meredith,' came the voice genuinely full of apology, the source now silhouetted with candles behind him.

Tentatively I reached out with my left hand, feeling the rough contours of the man's face beneath my fingertips.

Confident, I now had the range; I slammed my right fist

upwards with as much force as I could muster from the prone position I now found myself in. The blow failed to connect – my fist screaming just short of the man's head as he pulled back in alarm.

'Hey, it's me Mark, from the harbour. Do you remember me?'

Whether that comment was supposed to calm me down or not, I don't know. It just made me even more sorry that the haymaker I had thrown at him had missed and his head with its perfect features was still intact.

Apologising constantly, the muscular sailor lifted me with ease from the cold stone floor and helped me into one of the nearby cushioned wooden pews.

'I am so sorry Mr Meredith, are you all right?'

The look I gave him in response was certainly enough to answer the question without having to say a word. My hand instinctively went up to the injury on my head, instincts too made him pull away rapidly.

'I… I didn't know it was you,' he blurted, attempting, in vain I might add, to explain his course of action.

It was almost as if, that single comment would set things right between us.

'Well golly gee,' I replied, sarcasm and anger etched into each word. 'That makes everything so much better don't you think?'

In my mind it was obvious that this was not the case and in reality, this simple explanation was going nowhere near setting things right. Mark on the other hand, was simply either immune to sarcasm or was stupid beyond words.

'Well I'm glad we got that sorted, I thought you were going to be really pissed off when you woke up,' he replied, in the dim light I could just make out a smile.

'How long have I been out?' I asked, remembering Donald was monitoring the time for me.

'I didn't even know you were gay, but Judy did mention something which made me wonder,' he replied, his face dead pan, serious.

I looked at him for several seconds before clarifying the question, slowly.

'How long have I been unconscious?'

'About ten minutes, sorry,' he said looking down to the floor.

'Yeah, all right,' I mumbled. Then, something dawned on me, something he had said.

'What did Judy say?'

'Oh, nothing, sorry, perhaps you need to be in touch with your feminine side once in a while.' His smile returned.

'You're taking the piss aren't you!' I stated, realising that this dim-witted sailor was having a good laugh at my expense.

'Yes, sorry, just trying to cheer you up.'

'Well don't!' I snapped back.

Somewhere in the back of my head, just below where my hand was nursing a steadily growing hairy egg, a heavy metal drum solo was just winding itself up to a crescendo.

I thought that at any second, my skull was going to come apart, the pain and ringing in my head was making it a tough place for thoughts to hang out.

'What the hell...' I began in protest, then realising that I was, after all, in church stopped myself. 'Sorry,' I whispered. I do not believe in religion, that is true, but when in a religious place, it's best not to take chances. Just in case.

'Why did you hit me?' It seemed like a fair question to me. Mark leant closer to me.

'I thought it was him,' he replied in a whispered conspiratorial tone, cautiously now looking around the dimly lit church at the strange flickering shadows.

'Who's him?' I held my head harder, desperately trying to stop the pain and keep the broken bits of my skull from falling all over the church floor.

It didn't seem to be working. My right hand discovered a patch of stickiness on my forehead. Examining the palm of my hand in the flickering semidarkness, I could see a bright red smudge smeared across the fingertips and back up to the palm.

It took several seconds for my rattled brain to deduce that it was blood.

Mark had obviously struck me with something on the back of the head and in going down in a most undignified way like a sack of something floppy, I had hit my head probably on a pew end and now blood was leaking and oozing out of my shattered head from an assortment of holes, gashes, cuts and bumps.

A football sized lump seemed to be emerging from the wound on my forehead, the skin stretching awkwardly and adding to the tremendous pain and discomfort I was now feeling.

Mark shrugged. 'I don't know.'

I could see that I was getting nowhere fast, and with Mark's help, I would be attaining this level of progress for a while. Fun as it was, it would get old very quickly.

'Let's start again shall we?' I sighed.

He pulled a handkerchief from the pocket of his cut-off denim shorts and handed it to me.

In a masochistic way, I began to dab at the wounds I had so far discovered.

'Firstly, what are you doing here so late?' I asked.

'My grandfather, he lives down in the village with my grand-mother, she makes…' he began.

'Mark, let's just stick with your grandfather for the time being, shall we?' I prompted.

'Yes, if you insist.' He sat himself on the pew next to me.

'My grandfather is the caretaker here, has been ever since I can remember. Anyway, he's been ill for a few days now so I've been looking after things for him here when I've finished my chores in the harbour.'

'Okay, so secondly who did you think you were hitting when you slammed me in the head?'

'It's a long story.'

'Gets even longer if you don't bloody well start.'

'Well,' he began thinking back. 'It was perhaps a little after eight this evening. I was down in the vaults, they're only over there,' he indicated a barely visible doorway on the other side of the church. 'We have quite a few you know, like a maze some-times, Judy and I used to play down there.'

'Keep to the point, Mark.' Visions of Mark and Judy frolicking in the crypts of a church with generations of dead Dunnings looking on swam uncomfortably into my mind. It made me shudder.

'Anyway, I heard someone come into the church.' As I listened to Mark's account of his life story so far, I noticed he wasn't wearing a watch but decided that it was definitely not the best time to challenge him on that, it was probably an old sea dog trick to figure out what time it was by the way seagulls cawed or something like that.

'I thought it might have been Judy...'

'Why, why did you think it might have been Judy?' I asked returning to the conversation at the mention of her name.

'Oh, I don't know, we get on really well and she saw me down in the harbour earlier and said she might see me later.'

'Oh she did, did she?'

'Yes, well I thought it was either her or grandfather, so I came out to see. When I got up here, there was no one about but there were footprints by the door, they led over to the clock tower stairs.'

'Any pattern on the footprints by the door?'

'No, they were smooth soled ones.'

'What did you do with them?'

'Well, I had already tidied up in the church so the cleaning equipment was close by, so I mopped them up and quickly re-polished the floor there, I can see now that I'll have to do it again, Lord Dunning will be really angry if he comes in in the morning and sees that grandfather has not done his job properly.'

I decided that it was not a good idea to reveal the demise of Dunning at the moment.

'So, back to the footprints leading to the clock tower.'

'Yes.'

'Well?' I prompted again.

'Well, about a minute or so later he came down, it was one of the men I had brought across earlier from the mainland, one of Lady Dunning's weekend guests.'

'Who was he?' I asked, intrigued.

'I don't know, they all look the same to me, but I've seen him here before.'

'What in the church?'

'No, in the harbour last Wednesday, he said he had installed some surveillance equipment in case there was another robbery.'

'Burglary,' I corrected, 'another one?' I asked, suddenly latching on to what Mark had said.

'Yes, that's what he said.'

'Has there been a robbery, I mean a burglary before?'

He just shrugged.

'Well, did you go up and have a look at this surveillance equipment?'

I quickly examined the handkerchief, looking for a clean dry space on it for my dabbing to continue.

'No, he said it was sensitive gear and not to open the door.'

I raised myself shakily on to unsteady feet, using the edge of the pew as a support. I attempted to stand erect; something man has been doing for millennia, something I now thought was beyond me.

'Then he left,' Mark continued, 'said he'd be back tomorrow, and then he just went back to the house, or at least that's where I assumed he was going.'

'And that's why you hit me?' I looked down at a piece of six by four wooden baton, used for barring the church door from inside, one end was splintered and bloodied.

'Heavens no!' he replied, surprised that I had even considered such a thing.

'Oh, excuse me, so sorry. In that case what the bloody...' I had started to shout, infuriated by his lack of command of the most simple human ability to communicate clearly and concisely.

'Shh!' he interrupted, placing his right index finger against his lips.

I felt like slugging him, but I new full well that if I tried it, I would wind up flat on my face on the floor.

'He said that the robbers were still on the island and I should defend the surveillance equipment. As you didn't call out when you came in, I knew that you weren't him. I then saw you skulking about in the shadows, trying not to be seen, I thought that you must be one of the thieves, so I took up a piece of wood and was able to sneak up behind you and that's it. I only recognised you when you screamed.'

'I do not scream!' I contradicted stubbornly.

The tone in my voice challenged him to disagree. I thought for a second that he was going to, but then he just smiled.

'What have you been doing between this man leaving here and

you twatting me round the head with half a rain forest?'

He shrugged.

'I just went back down into the vaults and carried on, doing my chores, you know.'

'All right then, let's go and have a look at this surveillance equipment, perhaps it will tell us who we are dealing with here.'

Mark held out a muscular arm and, half carried, half pulled me through the old chapel arches and pillars, nooks and crannies to a flight of spiral old worn flagstone steps that, without light, disappeared up into the darkness above us.

'Any candles?' I asked, peering into the almost impenetrable blackness.

'No, it would be too dangerous, the passageway is quite narrow in places.'

'Any lights then?'

'Just my torch I'm afraid.'

Mark produced a small penlight sized torch from his belt and I aided him with my Maglite. Together, we were able to see well enough, and made our way up the stairs, the worn steps were wet with recently added mud. Mark was right though, no discernible tread, just wet muddy shoe shaped marks, stretched on ahead of us.

It took several minutes to ascend the circular stairwell. I was quite dizzy by the time we reached the narrow, short landing. My recent head injuries adding to my unsteadiness, the other side of this narrow, small platform, ended at a small, unlocked wooden door.

'This is the clock tower,' Mark stated, even he was labouring for breath.

Although not a very strenuous climb, it had seemed to be unending and my leg muscles were informing me that they would not appreciate doing it again anytime soon.

'When were you last up here?' I asked pointing to the door.

'Not for years,' Mark replied, looking towards the unlocked door.

'And your grandfather?'

'Not since the annual maintenance last February, the chapel is cleaned every night, some of the rooms, like the vaults and stuff are checked maybe twice a year, just to keep the rats out and make sure there is no damage or decay. But the clock tower, it only needs checking once a year and it is always done at the time of the routine maintenance,' he explained.

I sniffed the air, like some two-legged bloodhound. There was a sickly sweet odour lingering in the air.

It seemed to emanate from a pool of thick almost clear liquid that was collecting on the stone landing beneath the old rusty hinges on the right side of the door. I had no doubts as to its purpose.

'Oil.' I pointed out the pool with the beam of my torch. Reaching out I pushed the wooden door open. As I had noticed earlier, the door was unlocked, something that Mark had not observed, the fact seemed to surprise him.

'Grandfather always keeps this door locked, it's dangerous in there and the kids from the harbour are always sneaking in here, he wouldn't have left it unlocked,' he stated in disbelief.

'Mark, who has the keys for the clock tower?' I asked, already suspecting the answer.

'Only my grandfather and Lord Dunning, he has keys to all the doors in the church.'

The door swung back easily on the recently worked and oiled hinges in almost perfect silence.

Beyond the door, our torch beams revealed a cluttered and complicated room.

We found ourselves looking into a chamber occupied mainly with gears, cogs and spinning shafts. A huge opaque glass clock face was built into the wall of the tower opposite us, the overcast night sky outside allowing enough light into the chamber to enable us to see reasonably well, but I kept my trusty torch in hand, just in case.

I was about to step into the chamber when Mark's thick, muscle knotted heavy set arm stopped me dead in my tracks.

'What the hell did you do that for!' I snapped as his straight forearm caught me under the jaw, neatly clothes lined me.

'You have to be careful in here,' he warned, sounding like an old man reciting the mantra of behaviour to a young and disobedient child.

'Yes, I know that, lots of moving parts,' I sighed, attempting to push past him.

'Yes and no floor,' he casually observed.

I stopped and looked down, he was more or less right. Although there was no floor, there was a narrow wooden beam about eight inches wide. The beam was pitted with age and ran from the single narrow beam by the doorway across to the clock face, balanced on another narrow beam at its midpoint and another at its very end, I noticed with some concern, that the balanced beam was devoid of any secure point anywhere along its considerable length.

I guestimated that, from the beam, a knowledgeable person with a death wish could actually tinker with any mechanical part that needed adjustment.

The beam, by design, had no rails and no safety anchor points, if you fell it was a journey comprising of a short scream and ending when you became a wide, two-dimensional red smear on the flagstones of the church floor below.

The Health and Safety Executive would close this place down in a heartbeat.

'Be careful and follow me.' Mark walked, briskly and nimbly across the catwalk, his bulk causing the beam to creak and bounce ominously, threatening to send his massive frame earthbound, first class. He reached the clock face in about a dozen strides. On reaching the end of the beam, he turned and beckoned me across.

'Done this before?' I asked, playing for time, courage was in short order at the moment, and all the alcohol was back in the house.

'Once or twice,' he answered. 'Now come on, you can do it, be brave.'

I thought *patronising bastard*.

I leaned out of the doorway and looked down into the unwelcome, beckoning chasm below. Beneath the eight-inch wide beam I could see several bells hanging motionless. And about eighty feet beyond them I could just make out the altar.

'The secret is to remember, not to look down,' called Mark

from the other side of the chamber.

I noted that everyone says that when confronted with impending death through heart failure, or deceleration trauma caused by the poor victims current altitude and the distinct lack of terra firma, or a nice reassuringly solid substitute.

The most natural thing in the world for anyone of a nervous disposition to do is to ask why and then look down, ensuring to keep an eye fixed lovingly on what, in the next several seconds could be a hell of a lot closer and mark your untimely and extremely messy demise.

The pain in my head returned with a vengeance just to remind me of my currently weakened and dazed state. I switched off my torch and placed it carefully back into my pocket. And then, proudly, on hands and knees, in the most undignified manner I could imagine, I crawled across the chasm that was now opening beneath me.

Something moved across the heavens and the dim light from the moon vanished instantly. The only light in the clock tower machine room was coming from Mark's torch and the soft flickering light from the chapel far below me.

Occasionally, the lightning would flash again and in that brief moment of extreme brilliance that burst through the clock face, the silvery white light cast eerie and deep shadows, leaving me momentarily blinded when the flash faded. In those moments, I froze, too scared to move forward or back, Mark's voice the only constant. Reassuring me, urging me on.

When the fear had subsided, I crawled on, feeling my way forward across the beam, my eyes tightly closed; after all, what I couldn't see couldn't hurt me. Then I felt two rough spade-like hands on my shoulders, hauling me to my feet. With relief and surprise I realised that I had negotiated the maelstrom of spinning wheels, cogs and chains.

Firmly on my own two feet, I pulled out my torch and played its beam slowly around the clock tower. The beam of Mark's torch dissected the chamber in the other direction until it came to rest on a small black box, set against the clock face.

He nudged me with his elbow to gain my attention. On the edge of the precipice, he certainly got it.

'Watch it, for God's sake! I almost fell!'

'Sorry, is that what you're looking for?' His huge hand pointed into the torch beam with which he had trapped the small box in.

'Do you recognise it?' I asked, already knowing the answer.

He shook his head.

'In that case Mark, it may be just what we're looking for.'

Together, ducking and sidestepping the writhing, rhythmic clockwork mechanism, Mark and I negotiated our way along the narrow stone walkway at the clock face side of the tower, across to the box.

Hesitantly I reached out and picked it up. After all that I had endured, it was only a camera. It was a disappointment. I knelt down for a closer look, Mark doing the same, opposite me.

'Well?' he asked.

Well indeed.

It was a sophisticated device all right, state of the art with whistles and bells and all that. There was an output function on the box casing that seemed to be attached to a small aerial, obviously transmitting the images to some place nearby.

'It's a camera,' I sighed.

'A IRRMDC model 3,' Mark stated matter-of-factly, his eyes not moving from the camera casing.

I looked at him, in what I can only describe as awe, my jaw dropping down in disbelief. Was there more to this man than met the eye?

'What did you say?' I asked, my eyes never leaving him.

'It's an infrared remote controlled microwave digital camera model 3,' he stated confidently.

My father had told me about such things, a lot of the popular television investigative reporters used them, small, lightweight with an incredible picture quality and the ability to send images to a receiver miles away. Very expensive too, well out of the budget of most individuals, these things were bought and used by covert units for surveillance, the cameras being small, the lens could easily be as small as the thickness of a normal biro, perhaps even smaller.

'Mark, how did you know that?' My suspicions about the man were developing slowly, distrust and wariness edging into my voice.

'It's written on the side,' he replied looking straight at me, a blank expression on his face once more.

I released a deep sigh of relief, my original conclusion about the man remaining completely intact; he was still a yokel and nothing else. I checked, he was absolutely correct.

As I started to stand again, I noticed a length of thin metallic cord lying partially hidden beneath the edge of the remote camera housing. Carefully I pulled it free. It was about two feet in length and, as far as I could see, actually served no purpose in the room.

'What does all this do?' I asked, indicating the nearest and apparently slowest moving of the nearby cogs and gears.

Mark shone his torch beam over the mechanical unit and followed the gear shafts and cogs around the chamber before eventually telling me.

'It's the chime regulator.'

'What does it do?' I enquired, looking once more at the length of cord in my hand.

'It regulates the chimes,' he responded, shrugging as if the answer should have been obvious.

The man was trying my patience.

'Yes Mark, I had managed to work that out, but what does the chime regulator actually do?'

Mark thought for a few seconds and then began to explain.

'When the hands of the clock reach the half or hourly strike, the regulator releases the hammer and strikes the required number of chimes.' He was starting to sound like a teacher, instructing a slow and uninterested child.

But that was my job and I knew what he was now thinking.

'Okay, thanks,' I said cutting him off in midstream.

I could tell that he was about to give me a full description of the workings of the clock mechanism in microscopic and dull detail. 'Sounds pretty complex.' The statement, a privileged glimpse of the bloody obvious, strained at the back of my mind.

'Oh yes,' Mark acknowledged. 'My grandfather knows the workings of this clock inside and out, he taught me everything I know.'

'Couldn't have taken long,' I mumbled under my breath.

I stood up, another length of the metallic cord was entwined around what Mark had proudly described as the timing gear. I looked back at the broken cord in my hand and back at the wire that was wound tightly around the constantly moving cog, willing there to be some connection, something which would help me piece this murderous jigsaw together.

As I lazily rolled the cord between my fingers, I noticed a loop at one end of the broken cord, difficult to see under the limited artificial light. The cord must have been under considerable tension for some time to deform it like this.

'Okay,' I said after a few more minutes, 'I think I've seen everything that I need to up here. Let's go back downstairs.'

Mark led the way back across the aged beam, with me following cautiously not far behind. Back down the tower and then down into the chapel.

Once more back on terra firma, I looked down at my watch, Mickey, his smiling face and luminescent gloves, pointed out it was 12.45.

'Mark, can you come over to the main house first thing in the morning please, I need you to identify someone for me.'

'You mean the thief?' he asked in disbelief.

And murderer too, I thought.

'Maybe,' I replied.

'Sure,' he nodded enthusiastically, smiling happily.

'Anything to help, and once again, I'm sorry for hitting you.'

'Yes, it's all right, no real harm done,' I lied grudgingly, smiling back.

'Is it all right if I carry on with my chores?'

'Yes, I don't think there's much to be disturbed down here anyway.'

I left the church, allowing Mark to carry on his menial tasks, he seemed happy enough though.

Each to their own.

I made my way drunkenly across the lawn towards the dark brooding outline of the house.

By the time I had managed to stagger out of the church and reach the rose garden area, Mickey was pointing out it was one in the morning. Behind me, the lone toll of the church bell confirmed his estimation.

My throbbing head acknowledged the presence of the icy rain as relentlessly it poured down upon me.

The bright lights shone like stars from the otherwise empty darkness of the dining room and study windows. One or two of the lights on the second and third floors were on too, I knew, from my earlier exploration that these were the bedroom lights of some of the other guests.

My head injuries were enough to cause my slight disorientation. I noted that the path around the rose garden and I had parted company some time back, but as I could clearly make out the sleeping monolith of the Dunning residence, I used the nearest and brightest light as a beacon to home in on.

My attention was firmly fixed and focused when one of my feet, I think it was my left, caught in something hard and unyielding hidden in the darkness. I executed a perfect ten-point nosedive straight into the soggy turf of the croquet lawn landing awkwardly with a splash.

Groaning, I pushed myself back up into a kneeling position, the thought *this is just not my day* on the tip of my lips when I remembered Lord Dunning in the study. Perhaps I was wrong, perhaps some others were having a much worse day; I at least was still alive.

It was at this point that I noticed two deep rectangular imprints in the grass, deep and only now, from this almost prone position and the undignified angle with which I was now viewing the lawn, I saw them highlighted by the glare from the nearby window. The indentations were about fourteen inches apart, and as near identical as makes no odds.

I looked up, and saw an open window on the second floor, through which the sound of restrained, angry, disagreeing voices could be heard drifting on the night wind, however, these quarrelling voices were lost before I could fathom out as to whom they belonged.

I tried to stand, failed and fell back in the mud with another splash. I remembered my trapped foot and promptly set about disentangling myself from the croquet hoop to which I had somehow become attached.

Cautiously now, I edged slowly, backing my way to the rose bushes and then sidestepping gingerly along the edge of the garden – thus ensuring that I did not encounter any more half-hidden, hooped mantraps.

I was hopefully moving in the direction I believed the study door to be. After a few minutes, I knew I was right. All those years in the boy scouts had certainly paid off.

I squelched my way as quietly as possible through the study, the only occupant a dead lord who I had no chance of disturbing and I'm pretty sure he would not be moaning about the mess on his carpet from my muddy, crud covered training shoes.

And if by any mean feat he did have a complaint and tried to discuss it with me, I did not envisage being around long enough to witness the fact. But still I crept softly through the study and out into the hall, watching him nervously, just in case.

I pulled the study door closed to behind me gently, quietly so as not to disturb the other guests upstairs.

'Oh, you're back then?' The voice sounded next to my ear.

My heart and I nearly parted company, and not for the first time on this particular evening. I turned on the spot, spinning and lashing out, catching hold of Donald's lapels in my left fist. The lock, firm and restraining held him solidly in situ.

'What the hell do you think you are trying to do!' I hissed through tightly clenched teeth, attempting to control my suddenly released fear assisted rage. 'Are you trying to scare me to death?'

I didn't expect an answer to either question, and as expected, Donald did not offer to supply me with one.

I relaxed my grip and in doing so calmed down.

'Sorry,' he stammered in reply, visibly shaken. 'You were gone for such a long time, we were beginning to worry about you.'

'We?'

'Yes, we thought the murderer had struck again.' Donald brushed himself down and straightened the ruffled lapels of the penguin suit. 'Are you all right?' he asked, indicating my injuries. 'What's happened to your head?'

'Yes, I'm fine, thanks.' I have observed that it was always the same, if you ask an Englishman if he's all right, no matter what's the matter with him, or what crisis is currently destroying his life, wife left him, arm amputated, local pub closed down, he will never complain. It's not the English way, instead he'll reply, 'Yes, fine thank you.'

Judy would of course argue the point, '*men*' she said '*would complain of being near death when all they have is a cold.*'

I put it down to our English cultural upbringing, don't complain, suffer in silence.

I touched my head and discovered that the wound was still oozing rich, red blood but, I observed with some satisfaction, it had slowed.

'My head was mistaken for a baseball by an overzealous night watchman,' I said dabbing again at the leaking wound. I checked the handkerchief quickly for a clean spot to use to dab the wounds.

'Where?' Donald fished out a clean white handkerchief from his pocket, like a magician performing a magic trick, he handed it to me with a flourish.

'Thanks.' I accepted the offered makeshift bandage, and wondered how many more he had. 'The church,' I finally answered, 'Mark hit me although on reflection he didn't have a baseball bat, that would have been too simple. *No*, he used half a bloody tree.'

'Ouch!' winced Donald, visibly shuddering at the scene he was imagining.

'Yeah, bloody ouch. I think I may have been out of it for a while, but on the positive side, I think it increased his batting average.'

Donald didn't smile either.

'Do you need a doctor to look at that?' he asked, steering me towards the kitchen area.

'Have we got one?'

'No, Doctor Trevalian is still out looking for you, but we've got a first aid kit.'

'Close enough,' I conceded.

'Did you see any of the others?' Donald produced yet another pristine clean sparkling white handkerchief from his pocket, freshly cleaned, starched and folded. He handed this to me and I gratefully accepted it, discarding the already blood-soaked predecessor, placing this one firmly against the leaking lump on my swollen and distorted head. I grimaced with the pressure but the pain quickly ebbed away.

'No,' I replied. 'Who went out to find me?'

'Everyone,' he shrugged.

'Who exactly?'

'As I said, everyone, even the women came down and went looking for you, although they were told to stay together, just in case.' I could see a strong case for sex discrimination charging over the horizon towards him.

'Do you know where they went?'

He shrugged, 'No, I said that you may be in the garden, down by the church or the old harbour.'

'Oh, there you are,' came a disembodied voice from behind us. I turned to look back towards the study door that had opened soundlessly to see John Simmons and the major emerging from it.

It was the major who had spoken. 'In my old regiment you would have been up on a charge for disappearing like that.' The tone in his voice told me he was trying to scold me, like a naughty schoolboy.

I didn't care.

I amused myself by thinking how ridiculous he looked without his monocle, the smirk on my lips unintentionally obvious.

'It is no laughing matter, young man,' his voice rising a few octaves, a deep scarlet flush showing on his cheeks.

'It is from where I'm standing mate,' I replied, watching the vein in his neck pulsate violently.

'How dare you!' he snapped. 'In my old regiment…'

'Would you get put on a charge for beating the living shit out of stuck up majors in your old regiment?' I asked, interrupting his rhetoric of the old regiment.

'Yes of course,' he replied, as if the answer should have been obvious, even to a civilian like myself.

'Well, in that case major, I don't think I would have lasted that long anyway. Now get away from me before I prove the point to you!' The major's jaw dropped in astonishment.

'How dare you!' was his only response.

A few seconds later, while the major did his impression of a guppy on the bank, mouth flapping with nothing being said, Stanford and Drake came through the door behind them.

As a murder scene, the study was, forensically, a complete mess.

Both Drake and Stanford were bedraggled and soaked to the skin, they at least seemed glad to be back in the dry.

Either through the exertions of running and being hit, or the lateness of the hour, I yawned and realised for the first time just how tired I was. After a brief stopover in the kitchen, and being patched up with iodine and Elastoplast by Mary, with Donald's assistance I made my way upstairs.

'What can you tell me about that beach bum who drives the boats round here?' I asked, as we climbed the stairs.

'Who, Mark?'

'Yeah, obviously a good description.' I smiled.

'Not much to tell really.' He began, 'Mark lives down on the harbour with his grandfather Frank. Frank looks after the church.'

'What's he like though Donald?'

'No complaints, he's a good and conscientious worker, a little simple at times perhaps but he has a heart of gold, will do anything for anyone. He's even done some odd jobs around here if I've been too busy to tackle them.'

'Anything untoward recently?'

'Not really,' then something obviously occurred to him, trawling itself up from the depths of the back of his mind.

'Though just recently he has been a little forgetful, leaving ladders lying about outside.'

'Did he say why?'

'No, he of course denied it, swore blind that it wasn't him and that he always tidied up after himself.'

'Does anyone else use them?'

'No, there is no one else. There is only him or me who uses them, so who else could it have been?'

'Frank, perhaps?'

'No, besides Frank has been ill recently and Mark has been doing his own job during the day and Frank's job at night.'

'Obviously the extra workload is taking its toll.'

'Possibly.'

'What about his relationship with Judy?'

'What relationship?' he asked. 'They're just friends, grown up together. There's nothing else between them. Mark would never jeopardise his friendship with Judy, besides, he's madly in love with one of the trader's daughters, Nicky I think it is. She is away at the moment studying in London. I know that Judy and she are good friends.'

Happy to hear this, I relaxed a little. I had heard Judy on the phone to Nicky in the past but had never bothered to find out who this mysterious Nicky was, male or female.

Donald helped me into my room and I struggled to remove my muddy boots and damp clothing.

As he was leaving, I called out to him, 'Wake up call for eight, please.'

'In the morning?'

'Yes.'

Donald shouted something back but I didn't hear the response. My knees gave out. Sagging, I fell backwards on to the clean, laundered sheets. Mud, rainwater and blood all matted in my hair and on my body. I did not hear the door close as rest and peacefulness hit me like a wave. I slept in blissful contentment, oblivious to the events that had resulted in my exhausted state.

'Eight o'clock!' the strange voice at my shoulder yelled, slicing through the delicate veil of my peaceful dream like a red-hot razor through molten butter.

In an instant I was shocked into consciousness.

Sitting bolt upright, I was awake, refreshed and ready to tackle the hazards of a dozen soluble aspirin. My head was still pounding and ached with a passion that longed to be immediately quelled.

'Good heavens, you're very lively this morning after everything you went through yesterday,' said Donald.

I couldn't help but notice the black armband he was sporting on his left upper bicep.

He noticed me noticing it and said solemnly, 'Mourning.'

'Yes, morning to you too!' I managed to mumble.

He handed me a glass containing some foul looking fizzing and frothing brew.

I eyed it suspiciously. 'Any witches in your family?' I asked jokingly.

'No, sorry, no eyes of newt or anything like that I assure you,' he replied smiling at my attempt at humour. 'I thought you might need this.' He looked me up and down before giving his analysis, 'God, I was right, you look bloody awful.'

'Everyone else up?' I asked, my eyes never leaving the frothing brew.

'Doctor Trevalian was up at dawn, gone for a run he said. I told him about your little incident in the church last night, he said he'll look in on you later.'

'What about the others?'

'No, most of them are still in bed. Now drink this, you don't want to be frightening anyone do you?'

The way I was feeling at that particular moment defies explanation, needless to say though, I needed that level of reassurance and encouragement like I needed the proverbial hole in the head.

'Cheers.' I raised my glass in a mock toast, put the tumbler to my lips, closed my eyes and poured the contents bravely into my mouth. I was right about the taste too; it struck the back of my dry, parched throat and slid down like a frothing slimy lump. It not only looked foul, it tasted worse, like drinking fizzy chalk.

Instinctively I pulled a face, grimacing and almost retching. The fizzing bitter taste faded quickly leaving a refreshing, revitalised feeling that spread rapidly through my aching limbs.

'Old family recipe,' said Donald smiling, collecting the now empty tumbler from me. It took several seconds before I was able to speak again, but I felt a whole lot better.

'Is Mark here yet?' I was aware of a dull ache emanating from my jaw and I guessed that Mark's wild but ever so successful swing had done more damage to my face than I had at first realised.

'No. Why? Are you expecting him?' Donald placed the glass on a neat silver tray on the dressing table by the door.

'Yes, I asked him to meet me here first thing this morning.' I swung my legs out of bed and sat up on the edge of the bed.

A deep frown raced across Donald's face, 'That's odd.' He shrugged dismissively and made to leave, in a second I was across the room, restraining him gently but firmly with a tug on his arm.

'Why? What do you mean odd?'

'Well, it's just that first thing in the morning for Mark is about six o'clock,' he replied.

'Perhaps he's overslept,' I suggested.

'Mark? Not a chance.' Donald obviously set great store by Mark's punctuality and although he was not my favourite of people, I had noticed that he did seem to have an air of reliability about him.

'Can we phone his grandfather, see if he's on his way up here or if he's maybe doing some more chores?' I asked, releasing Donald's arm.

'Normally I'd say yes, but unfortunately, none of the phones on the island have been working since the burglary last week. Lord Dunning has,' he stopped himself, 'had,' he corrected, 'been in touch with the telephone company, a repair team are due tomorrow.'

'All right then, can you go over to his place and get him, I need to speak to Judy.'

'Yes, of course, I'll take the car, I should only be ten minutes or so.' Donald started to leave and I stopped him again.

'Ten minutes?'

'Yes.'

'How come it took so long to get up here Friday night then?'

'You came by buggy,' he explained, 'the other road is too steep for the buggy but the four-by-four can cope with it a lot easier, besides, it was supposed to be a romantic interlude for you and Miss Judy.'

'Lady Dunning's idea?' I asked, crossing back to the window and pulling open the curtains. Daylight flooded into the room, making me wince with the brightness.

'Who else.'

I heard Donald open the bedroom door and walk out on to the landing. 'By the way, it's stopped raining, it's a beautiful day, have a shower and join the rest of the human race.'

I heard Donald laughing as the door swung shut behind him.

A quick glance to the full-length mirror in the corner of the room confirmed what I was already feeling. I looked a mess but I resigned myself to the fact that it was becoming a habit.

The shower was glorious.

I felt fully revived from the neck down, the fizzing potion and the hot invigorating water jets had massaged away the aches and pains from my battered and tortured body. From the neck upwards it was of course another story entirely. It felt as if I had no skin on my face, the water jets slicing violently across the lumps, bumps and cuts, the pain erupting once more, reminding me that this was definitely the morning after the night before.

My skin, stretched tightly across my skull, seemed to have shrunk overnight, keen on covering all the bruises and swellings that were happily forcing themselves up from the bones that felt soft and tender to the touch. I was sure that my mouth had been pulled up and to the right, my jaw muscles ached and I noticed that my jaw bone itself seemed to click every time I opened and shut my mouth; this I found quite disconcerting, so forced myself to stop doing it after a few attempts.

I dressed quickly, combing my hair carefully, wincing as the many sharp, viscous teeth of the metal comb raked over new wounds I was only just discovering. The shave, thankfully, did not happen; I was already in enough pain.

I sat down next to Judy and quietly began working my way through the eagerly anticipated breakfast treat. I was painfully aware of the daggers in Judy's eyes repeatedly stabbing me as I began to indulge in the mammoth cholesterol loaded fry up. I managed one, maybe two mouthfuls, but the enjoyment was already gone and I reluctantly gave up; the pain in my bruised and swollen jaw proving to be an ally of Judy's disdain after all.

I tried a smile, just to put her at ease. Once again I found this even harder than eating.

Judy placed her hand firmly on my knee, squeezing it reassuringly, 'Cole, what happened to you?' Genuine concern in her voice, she reached up to my battered and distorted forehead with a white linen napkin and gently touched my tender brow. The pain shot through my head like an express train.

'Jesus, Judy! That hurts like hell!' I tried, without upsetting her, to ensure that she didn't touch my fractured head again.

'I'm sorry. I was only trying to help. What happened to you?'

I was aware of slightly more free movement in my jaw.

'Your friend Mark, that's what happened to me.'

'What... What do you mean?'

'Mark, he slugged me,' I explained.

'Why?'

'When?' asked the major from the other end of the table. I looked across at him in disbelief. His monocle once more wedged firmly in place, silver and sparkling in the sunlight from the windows behind him.

'Er... Last night, remember?' sarcasm lost on him once more. 'I went out. You all went looking for me. I came back sporting these two black eyes and these lumps on my head.'

'Yes, yes of course, how stupid of me to forget.' He smiled and helped himself to another cup of tea.

'I asked you why?' Judy repeated, folding her arms and giving me her patented *tell me everything now* stare.

'Mistaken identity,' I replied simply. 'Anyway, how are you and your mother coping?' I continued, quietly, reassuringly turning to Judy.

'Mother is very upset of course, but I think she's coming to terms with what's happened.' She sighed.

'Yes, but what about you?'

'Oh, I'm all right. I'm looking after mother so I haven't really had time to think about it. Keeping myself occupied seems to keep my mind off the whole ghastly thing.'

'Judy, you can't hide away from it forever, your father is dead, you have to face it sometime.'

'I know that Cole, but I don't want to talk about it now.'

'Excuse me young man.' Lady Barton was frantically waving at me from the other end of the table; even now she was still dressed in her finest clothes. I could imagine her saying something about maintaining standards in any given situation, not letting the side down and all that.

'What time are the police due? Bopsey is all alone with my housekeeper and she worries so.'

'I'm sure your housekeeper won't be worried for too long.'

She looked back at me blankly, and then realisation dawned on her. 'Oh you silly boy, I'm not talking about the silly house-keeper. Bopsey will be worried, makes a terrible mess when she's worried.'

I could see Lady Barton about to give us a lecture on the trials and tribulations of being a pampered poodle owner and a responsible parent. Before I could answer though, Donald suddenly burst through the dining room doors, red faced and gasping, his dramatic crashing entrance causing the double doors to swing wildly back into the room.

The ladies and I jumped in startled alarm.

'Mr Meredith, Cole, can I have a word with you please.' It sounded like an offer I didn't want to refuse.

I made my excuses and Donald and I went back into the hall. I closed the dining room door behind me.

'What is it?'

Donald seemed agitated and not just because of his breathless condition.

'It's Mark,' he wheezed, 'he hasn't shown up at the harbour or his grandfather's place.'

'Perhaps he met this girl Nicky last night whilst walking home and got lucky, stranger things happen,' I suggested, trying to steer my vicious thoughts away from what else could have happened. 'Or perhaps because of the weather last night, he decided to stay in the church.'

Donald nodded enthusiastically, 'Yes, you're right, I think we should go and check, are you coming?' Before I could answer, Donald was already halfway across the hall and into the study. Shrugging, I resigned myself to follow the butler.

Lord Dunning was beginning to ripen, the sickly-sweet smell of death and decay was now permeating everything. I wished we could move him someplace to keep him fresh, but I knew the police, whenever I could figure out how to contact them, would want the body left where it fell, or in this case where it slumped.

As we reached the shattered, wide-open French doors, the

hallway door opened behind us.

'Don? Mr Meredith? Are you in there?' Mary called. I noticed she was using the door as a shield to protect her precious eyes from witnessing the corrupt and broken body of her former employer. Donald turned and went back to his wife, using his body as a bonus shield to restrict her view further.

'Don't come in here, Mary.' It was more than a suggestion. I noticed the delicate hint of care in his voice, Mary must have noticed it too, he had her best interests at heart and she knew it. 'What do you want?'

'It's… It's Mr Carpenter, he hasn't come down for breakfast and I can't wake him, he won't answer his door.'

Donald turned his face to me, shrugging. 'Should we check it out?'

'Yes.' I was already walking back to the happy couple. 'I think perhaps we better had.'

Tim Wolfe was already outside Carpenter's bedroom doorway as Donald, Mary and I reached the landing. Wolfe was crouched before the threshold, like some great anthropomorphic boulder paying homage to the door.

'Wolfe?' I called as I saw him.

'Door locked… Nearly got it.' He spoke in broken, short sentences, concentration etched into his face.

As I neared, I saw that he was dragging a newspaper from beneath the narrow gap beneath the door. After several seconds of gently easing the paper back towards him, a small silver door key emerged, carried triumphantly in the centre of the tabloid press.

Wolfe picked the key up in his monstrously over inflated hand and forced himself upright, raising himself to his full height, his knees clicking and crunching in protest at the effort forced upon them.

'Got it.' Wolfe smiled maniacally, a self-congratulating smile, acknowledging his own resourcefulness and ingenuity as he turned and held his recently won prize out to us. I took the key from him and pressed it fully into the keyhole, a half-turn clockwise and the reassuring sound of the lock releasing was our own reward.

With Wolfe standing on my left, Donald on my right and him urging Mary to stay well back, I pushed the door open. Inside, the heavy curtains were drawn tightly closed and the lights were on. The smell of death lingered in the enclosed room, faint but now all too familiar.

Without stepping into the room, I knew death lay beyond the threshold.

I called back, 'Mary, find Doctor Trevalian, bring him here please.'

Without question, she was gone, her lithe frame vanishing silently down the corridor like a ghost.

'What's that smell?' asked Wolfe, whispering into my ear so as not to disturb anyone. Out of the corner of my eye, I saw his face screwing in disgust.

'Death,' mumbled Donald, turning away and hanging his head.

'No, not that. I know what death smells like.'

I took a quick sniff of the musty air. He was right, beneath the sickly cloying stench of death, there was another smell, faint, like rotting vegetation.

Cautiously, I stepped forward into the room. As I took my third tentative step forward, the thick carpet beneath my foot released an unexpected squelching noise, liquid oozing over the top of my shoe. I looked about me; the room was clean, tidy. Nothing noticeably out of place.

Slowly, I turned, looking around the open door, there, just out of sight I saw him.

The crumpled body of Stephen Carpenter, ex-solicitor of this parish was still dressed in his formal evening wear from the previous night. A crystal glass tumbler still clutched in his right hand, a shattered glass decanter by his left, the contents of which had escaped and had caused the oozing, squelching pool, in which I was currently standing. Carpenter's skin was waxy in appearance, his face and hands a cyanosis blue, his eyes, bulging and wide open staring toward the ceiling, focused on nothing. His mouth open at an awkward, unnatural, unliving angle, the blood around his teeth and lips continued evidence of his suffering in his final throes of death. His body appeared to have slumped into its current position rather than fell, judging by the strange position of his legs twisted beneath him.

Wolfe called enquiringly from the doorway, 'Well?'

'He doesn't look too well,' I called back, crouching next to the old man's contorted body. I reached out and checked for a pulse, a sign of life. After several seconds, the coldness and rigidity of the man's neck caused me to withdraw my hand without finding a beat.

'I think Michael needs to be here.'

'I'm here, what is it?' Michael Trevalian crashed into the room, his sudden arrival sending Tim Wolfe sprawling out in the hallway and causing me to jump with a start.

'It's Carpenter, we found him like this.' I stepped back and let the professional take over.

Quickly he went to work, producing a small torch attached to his key fob. He pushed and prodded the immobile solicitor, flashed the small torch beam into the man's eyes and sniffed at the man's mouth. A look of uncertainty, confusion, developed into disbelief as he began to attempt to remove the man's clothing.

'What is it?' asked Wolfe from the doorway. 'What have you found?' Wolfe's restraint and refusal to engage in matters of the dead, without a good story ensuring he maintained a vigil from the corridor, where from his position by the door, could hear but not see the scene Trevalian and I were playing out.

'I've seen this before,' Trevalian continued, his careful removal of the man's clothing continuing, unsuccessfully but optimistically. The stiffness in the solicitor's limbs made the task difficult to impossible.

'Where?' I asked, looking again into the obviously dead man's milky, bulging eyes.

'Columbia.'

'Is he dead?' asked Wolfe quietly, again from behind his wooden shield.

'He better be, I'd hate to look like this and still be alive,' mumbled Trevalian, struggling with the man's left arm.

'How long?' I asked, stepping back from the body.

'I'd say about twelve hours, certainly no less.'

'How can you be so sure?' Wolfe's voice was laden with suspicion.

'Fixed lividity of the skin, cloudy corneas and, as you can probably tell,' grunted Trevalian in reply, again trying to remove the dead man's jacket, 'full body rigidity.' He gave up and sat back on his haunches, sweating.

'What about cause of death?'

'Cole, I can't be sure but...'

'Natural causes?' volunteered Wolfe. I knew he was now edging for another scoop.

'No, I don't think so.'

Wolfe was around the door and with us, peering ghoulishly over the body before Trevalian had finished speaking.

'So what? Is he supposed to be that colour?'

Trevalian sighed, 'No, it looks like asphyxia or choking.'

'Strangled then?' Already the cogs of the front page were running in Wolfe's imagination.

'No,' I interjected before Trevalian could respond. 'There are no ligature marks on the neck, no signs of forced entry, the door was locked from the inside with the key still in the lock, you told us that yourself.'

Wolfe became silent for several seconds, thoughts racing through his mind, his eyes rapidly moving from side to side as he quickly evaluated what was being said. Then, in a flurry of movement that belied his ample size, he crossed the room to the heavy curtained windows and dramatically threw the drapes back. The windows, now revealed, were all closed, locked, the key on the windowsill beneath the locked frames.

'And the windows locked too,' I concluded. I turned back to Trevalian, 'Michael, what are you looking for?'

Doctor Trevalian had again begun to try removing the dead man's jacket, he was proving again to be without success.

'Injection marks,' he wheezed.

'Why?'

'As I said, I've seen this a lot in Columbia, natives there called it the flying death.'

Wolfe stopped in his tracks, hardly moving as he hissed, 'Bugs?'

'No, poison tipped arrows.'

Wolfe sighed with obvious relief, 'Just got to keep a look out for Tonto then.' He went back to the window and stared out across the croquet lawn to the church. 'Shouldn't be that hard to spot.'

'It looks like curare, a vegetable based poison, causes instant death, the victim dies of asphyxia as the lungs are paralysed.'

'What makes you think it's curare?' I asked. I had heard of the poison being used by serial killers, usually doctors who were after a quick end to their nemesis, but I knew little more about it than it needed to be injected.

'I don't know for certain, but it's the only poison I know that produces these symptoms and acts instantly.'

'How do you know it acted instantly?'

'Look how he's fallen, he's just collapsed, sagged.'

'That doesn't make sense,' I replied, shaking my head.

'Why?'

'Well if it was instant, the person administering the poison would be in the room, right?'

'Yes.'

'So where are they? The room was locked from the inside, there are no ways out of the room, the murderer should still be here.'

'Suicide,' concluded Wolfe, still looking out of the window across the picturesque landscape.

'So the needle would still be in him,' I sighed.

'Which it isn't,' stated Trevalian, after a brief and fruitless search.

'Perhaps,' said Wolfe, turning to face us, a triumphant look on his face, 'perhaps he's swallowed it, in the food or drink earlier.'

I looked with great suspicion on the ruins of the decanter. Trevalian shook his head in dismay, 'Sorry, no, curare is harmless if swallowed, it has to be injected into the bloodstream, otherwise, no effect, just a bitter aftertaste.'

'Well, there's nothing else here.' Wolfe turned back to the window, 'So now what?'

'I'm not sure, you and Michael check the room out, see if we've missed anything at all, then lock it. Don't tell the others yet. Donald and I are going to check out the church, see if Mark spent the night there. With any luck, we shouldn't be long.'

By the time Donald and I had reached the marsh-like croquet lawn, we were both at full sprint, mud and grass splashing up our legs as we raced across the garden. In bright sunlight, it was easy now to avoid the metal croquet hoops. Down the rocky uneven shale path, through the neat rose gardens and into the old churchyard.

As soon as we reached the low walled boundaries of the church, I had a clear and unobstructed view of the church doors, instantly I could tell something was badly amiss. Initially I was unsure as to what had actually alerted me, perhaps the odd smell carried on the morning sea air, the strange, brooding, haunting silence.

Looking back, with the certainty of twenty-twenty hindsight, I know now that it was the unexpectedly open church door. Leaves and other wind carried debris were strewn about not only in the usually well maintained church porch but across the stone threshold and inside the church too. From my brief encounter with Mark, the meticulous and conscientious, I knew that he would never have deliberately left the door open, unless something was terribly terribly wrong. The sickening, sinking and tightening feeling in my gut increased in intensity as I neared the church door. Together, Donald and I reached the heavy wooden doors in unison.

They were several inches ajar.

A flashback from the previous night came shuddering back into my mind with crystal clarity and painful alarm and so, I courageously stepped aside, allowing Donald to be first across the church threshold. Reassuringly, no one lashed out at him with ferocious murderous intent. Happy in this realisation, I deduced it was safe to enter and followed quickly behind him.

I looked down, and saw that a muddy set of featureless, smooth footprints led away into the dark recesses of the church, the prints were the same as I had witnessed outside the church the previous evening. On entering the cold body of the church, none of the sinister, unnerving atmosphere of the previous night had gone. In fact, in the cold light of day, the feeling of being totally out of place washed over me with a vengeance.

The hairs on the back of my neck prickled with foreboding.

Several of the candles in their ancient black iron sconces off to my left were fresh and unlit, as if Mark had replaced them but had not, as yet got around to lighting them. Others near the door stood limp and blackened. Defeated sentinels of the dark.

The way the candles had been burnt on one side more than the other, led me to suspect that their flames had been extinguished by the sea winds in the night. I concluded that the heavy church doors must have been open for most of the night. These oak doors, far too heavy for the winds to open alone, I suspected the hidden hand of a human agent.

Cautiously, I checked more of the sconces, especially those situated well away from the door. The candles here had burnt to the stump. Molten tallow solidified whilst overflowing their reservoirs.

The stained glass warriors and angels, encased within the ancient leaded bars of their decorative prisons, stared down upon us with a look that could easily have been interpreted as contempt as we moved slowly, methodically about our prying, curious business.

'Over there!' Donald's yell snapped me back to our current situation.

He pointed to a pile of ragged clothing on the stone floor beneath the bell tower, half hidden in the dark shadows.

'Mark!' I mouthed the name, the words trapped in my throat never quite being heard. Together, Donald and I ran to the misshapen form, broken and twisted on the cold tiled debris strewn floor.

The body, face down, was cold and deathly pale, the eyes, what was left of them, were wide open and staring. A deep crimson puddle had formed and coagulated around his open shattered mouth, another spread from his eviscerated stomach. What was left of the poor man's head was little more than shattered gristle and bone.

The ruin of his face little more than a broken shell.

The crimson tendrils of his life blood had reached out to the fingers of blood from his mouth, and had formed a thickening, crusty river of rich, red fluid, which had cascaded down the steps of the vestry and down into the cracks between the tiles.

Both of Mark's dead hands were tightly clenched at arms length in front of him, as if in a futile attempt to fight off his murderous assailant.

Mark's broken corpse was bleached white.

Through the cold night he had lain here, probably waiting for someone to find him, to help him, no one had come. It sickened me that in this holy place, this man's prayers still went unanswered.

He had died alone, without hope.

Donald and I were crouched low over the man's body in grieved, stunned silence. Tentatively I reached out a hand to find the carotid pulse in his neck. The intense cold and stiffness of the body threw my probing fingers away.

'He's dead,' I announced quietly.

'You think?' Donald mumbled looking at me in what I assumed was disgust.

It was a fact both Donald and I were aware of, but now, in saying the few words, the reality and finality really struck home.

A shaft of early morning sunlight glinted off something near the body, it was small but the sparkle caught my attention instantly, thin slivers of bloodied glass reflected in the refracted sunbeams. I looked hard at the shimmering line on the floor, tracing a short snaking line towards the dead man's hand.

I saw that Mark was clutching a thin chain of a gold coloured metal in the tightly bunched fist of his left hand. With a little not so gentle persuasion, he was convinced to part with it.

It appeared to be a small golden coloured bent and warped circlet of metal, crushed in the dead man's grip, it was about an inch and a half in diameter, it was badly distorted due to the intense pressure that had been applied to it during Mark's last moments of life; as he struggled with his assailant in a desperate battle for his life.

In the other hand, after a little more persuasion, Mark revealed his final secret, a small, single brass metal cylinder, open at one end, the smell of raw burnt cordite which emanated from the spent brass cartridge was almost overpowering. I recognised the item immediately, it was nothing less than a fired casing, judging by its size, probably from a 9mm automatic pistol. At a guess, I imagined that the spent round had been ejected into the darkness of the church.

'He's been shot,' whispered Donald, 'twice.'

From the shape of what remained of Mark's head, and the large punched out hole in his chest, it was easy to see that the poor lad had most definitely been shot, first in the back from close range, the skin around the obvious entry wound in the boy's lower back. Against his ribs was burst open a ragged star shape, denoting a point blank shot. As the boy lay writhing in agony, already dying. He had tried crawling away from his assailant, clawing desperately for life, his murderer had simply walked up behind him and fired a single round through the back of his head, executed.

I found myself asking again and again, *Why*?

What did he know?

What did he see?

What had brought such a terrible end to this poor lad's simple life?

In my heart, I knew the answer lay back in the large house, now more a mausoleum than a home, but the answer must be there.

'Come on Donald, I've seen enough. We have a date with a murderer, and I can't wait to put this bastard right where he belongs.'

I stood up and pulled the reluctant Donald up after me. He followed me for several steps, stopped and returned to the body. Slowly, he removed his jacket and placed it gently over the dead boys broken corpse.

Then, he bowed his head in silent prayer and crossed himself. He turned and walked slowly over to where I was waiting by the church doors.

He shrugged, 'It seemed the right thing to do,' as he pushed past me into the morning sun.

I nodded in agreement, closing the church doors behind us.

The journey back to the house seemed to take an eternity. Slowly we trudged along the path, through the rose garden and across the lawns.

The whole situation with Mark had hit us both harder than either of us was prepared to let on.

I found myself lost in desperate thoughts, Dunning, Carpenter, Mark, who was going to be next? Judy, me? The murderer needed to be caught before the answer was a mute point.

Neither Donald nor I wanted to be the first to break the strained silence that now hung obtrusively in the air between us.

It sounds corny, I know, but I felt that this time belonged to the dead, the victims of this faceless killer. Admittedly, I didn't know Mark very well, I hadn't known any of them for long, and in all honesty, I can't say any of us would ever have been great friends, but no one deserves to die like that. No one.

The contaminated, spoilt and trampled murder scene was our point of entry back into the house. The study doors wide open.

Still in silence, we skirted around the bloody corpse of Lord Dunning, his massive frame now barely hidden by the covering curtain, the unmistakable odour of death now heavy and cloying in the morning air.

As I crossed the room, out of the corner of my eye, I saw movement. My attention was instantly drawn to it, like a doomed moth to an inviting flame. Lying partially hidden beneath Lord Dunning's desk, I saw several pages from an A4 typed manuscript.

I was sure that I would not have missed something obvious like this, in the morning sunlight, the papers fairly shone. I knew that on my previous explorations around the office I had not seen them, and when leaving the study for the church not so long ago, these papers were not present, sure I had seen muddied and spoilt papers but nothing so bright as these A4 sheets.

I reached out, and picked them up, each one of the manuscript pages were clean, crisp and clear, each one headed simply YORKS PROJ#456.

I looked around the floor with renewed vigour.

Yes, there were still other papers, muddy and wet now, covered with numerous footprints, the contents of which were smudged and spoilt. Obviously those had been on the floor for a while, and it was conceivable that in the poor light, I may have missed some of these muddied papers, hidden amongst the filth and dirt that had been trudged through the room by all and sundry.

I checked the desk drawers in front of Lord Dunning. I was surprised to discover all bar one of them was now unlocked.

'Donald, who else has keys for these desk drawers?'

'No one,' he replied stopping at the study door to the hallway and turning back. 'Lord Dunning was very particular about that. He had the only key. He never kept duplicates. He confided in me once, that all his Achilles heels and private schemes were kept in there, he didn't want any unscrupulous git to get hold of them, he thought it might ruin him if any of his more unpopular projects were discovered by the pond life.'

'Pond life?'

'Yeah, that was his lordship's generic term for anyone who wasn't up to his level of evolution in the social jungle.'

'Nice. Okay, in that case, where did he keep the desk drawer keys?'

'I don't know,' he replied, shrugging, 'but Mary was always dusting in here and she never found a key, she would have told me. I suppose he must have kept it somewhere close to him, somewhere he could keep an eye on it.'

I found myself thinking along the lines of *if I was a key, where would I be*. It didn't help.

'If you had a secret, that you didn't want anyone else to know, what would you do?' I asked Donald, my own thoughts racing to get an answer to the question I had just thought about aloud.

After several long seconds in deep, silent calculating thought, Donald shook his head and sighed, 'I don't think I would keep any incriminating documents if their discovery meant losing everything and going to jail.'

'No,' I conceded, 'me neither, but, if it was for business purposes, you would need them to ensure that no one screwed you all ways from Sunday wouldn't you.'

'Like an insurance policy?'

'Exactly, insurance against a double cross.'

Donald thought about this for a few seconds before finally nodding the affirmative. 'Yes, I suppose so.'

'So you would want to keep the information under lock and key.'

'Yes,' he again agreed.

'And you would keep the key to this lock very safe.'

'Yeah, I wouldn't let it out of my sight.'

'No you wouldn't, would you, you would keep the key on you at all times.'

Quickly I crossed to Dunning's body, and snatched back the curtain shroud, catching a strong fragrance of death on the sea wind. I swallowed hard and started to search the dead man's pockets. At last, success, a small brass key lay in a handkerchief in the dead man's breast pocket. Cautiously, I removed the key and inserted it carefully into the lock of the only drawer still secured against invasion. A perfect fit.

A gentle twist and CLICK.

Slowly, I drew open the drawer, another pile of A4 leaves of paper all headed YORKS PROJ#456 lay secure within.

The gentle sea breeze skittered through the French windows behind me, agitating the now revealed pile of headed notepaper. Several pages of the document were picked up by the delicate, invisible fingers of the morning breeze, they floated freely on the early barely perceived winds, picked up gently from the open wooden drawer and carried slowly to the carpeted floor beneath the desk.

I opened the drawer to its fullest extent, and there, at the very back of the drawer I saw what I was looking for. What I considered to be the missing piece of the jigsaw. The clue which neatly bound everything together.

It was small, but it was definitely there.

A small, barely visible, shining globule of grease and the distinct perfume of oil on the papers inside the drawer confirmed my theory.

Now, to announce it.

'Come on Donald, it's time to unveil our killer.' I smiled triumphantly, pulling the curtain back over Dunning's head.

'You know who did it?' he asked open-mouthed, shock and

surprise in his voice.

'Yes of course, but it's more than that isn't it?'

Donald looked at me bemused.

I continued in answer to his unasked question, 'Well, there are several questions we can now answer.'

'Several questions?'

'Oh yes,'

'What questions?'

'Firstly, who was the burglar who stole the rifle, and what purpose was the weapon stolen for?'

'You know that?'

I nodded.

'Do you know who killed Lord Dunning?'

'Yes, and Stephen Carpenter and Mark and more importantly, why.'

I counted the questions off on my fingers, the bemused look on Donald's face never shifting.

'And you can answer all those questions?'

'I can!' I stated confidently. 'Now Donald, I need you to get everyone together and I do mean *everyone*.' I stressed the point. 'Ask Tim Wolfe and Doctor Trevalian to meet me here and then get everyone else into the drawing room as quickly as you can, with any luck, we'll be back on the mainland by lunchtime.'

'You've got it.' Donald left the room at a run, pushing the door closed behind him.

I had preparations of my own to make.

I crossed to the small drinks table in the corner of the room; it was sturdy and well made. Carefully I removed the items adorning its highly polished surface, placing these items, a decanter, several tumblers and an empty ice bucket on to the study floor.

I picked up the table and walked, awkwardly, struggling with the considerable weight over to the bookcase. I reached up, and pushed in the leather bound, dusty volume entitled *Great Shoots of Britain* as I had seen Lord Dunning do, only yesterday, it now seemed a lifetime ago.

As before, the bookcase swung back silently. I struggled into the now revealed walkway with the table. Reaching the stairway, I stepped on to the first step and then, with all my might, threw the table forward and down the unyielding stone steps.

The table disintegrated under its own momentum, shattering heavily at the base of the stairs.

I turned hastily and ran back to the now closing bookcase, with a tremendous effort and a leap any rugby player would have been proud of, I dived headlong through the narrowing gap, rolling and regaining my feet, back in the study.

Surprisingly, Donald returned to the study a little under fifteen minutes later, Wolfe and Trevalian, now casually dressed in denim and shirts, were with him.

'As requested,' Donald announced, closing the door behind him, precautions against prying ears or curious eyes.

'And the others?' I asked, perching myself on the arm of the large, leather bound chair which usually faced Lord Dunning's now shattered desk.

'All making their way to the drawing room even as we speak. Lady Dunning had to be quite firm with a few of the guests.'

'Really?' I asked, curiously. 'Which ones?'

'The Simmons and Lady Barton actually, they're not happy about staying here a moment longer than absolutely necessary and they can't see the point of them meeting anywhere, just to be accused, and I quote, *of being a cold blooded killer* unquote,' smiled Donald. He adopted his usual pose, relaxed, arms behind back, standing almost motionless beside the door.

'All right, Cole,' sighed Wolfe, sitting himself in a high backed, uncomfortable looking wooden chair, well away from the curtain-shrouded corpse. 'Your boy here said you wanted the good doctor and myself here. Why?' Wolfe tried to make himself comfortable, but due to his size exceeding the design specifications of the small chair, he appeared to be finding it difficult. In the end, he settled for crossing his legs, his left hand clamping on to the right shin as it rested heavily on his left thigh.

The antique chair creaked ominously in complaint of the extra, unwanted load.

'Tim, you followed the Dunning paternity case in court quite closely, didn't you?' I asked, turning slightly on the padded leather arm of the chair, a low, rumbling squeak ensued, which caused a wry smirk from Trevalian and Wolfe. Donald, professional to the last remained stony faced.

'Sure did, it was a bit of a farce if the truth be known.' He shrugged.

'Did you ever meet the complainant?'

'No, never did, she always remained behind a screen, something that Lord Dunning insisted on. She was just some bint with no taste, nothing special, I'm sure.'

I nodded, acknowledging but not necessarily agreeing with what he said.

Lord Dunning himself had requested her identity to be kept secret, not the usual approach for an uncaring, unemotional businessman.

'And of course, the retraction at the end of the case and the court costs levied against her,' added Wolfe, suddenly remembering little snatches of the story. 'Carpenter was dealing with that, so he must have known who she was.'

'Michael,' I turned my attention to the doctor, still standing, arms folded, feet apart braced midway between Wolfe and myself. 'You performed the paternity tests?'

'That's right, yes, Carpenter bought the blood samples to me for analysis.'

'Did you ever meet the alleged mother?'

'No, only the blood samples.'

'What were your findings?'

Trevalian stepped away, moving slowly closer to the door. 'I can't tell you that Cole.'

I shrugged, 'Fair enough.'

He stopped and looked at me, his brow lined with deep furrows as he frowned, 'That it? You're not going to pry further?'

'No,' I sighed. 'No need, I was just trying to tie up a few loose ends, that's all. I already have all the answers I need to prove who stole the weapons, killed Carpenter, Dunning and Mark.'

Wolfe, smiled widely. 'You too.'

I nodded and stared him straight in the eye. I found myself wondering again, had the hack beat me to the punch, was he about to prove me wrong, an investigative journalist with perception. I knew they existed. I didn't think Wolfe fell into that

145

category.

'What's your theory, Tim?'

'It was the Simmons's wasn't it!' he announced, smiling smugly. 'I knew it right from the start.'

'Why? Why would it be them?' asked Michael, his eyes darting quickly from Wolfe to me and back again.

'Revenge,' he shrugged, 'pure and simple, revenge for the death of their daughter Lucy. Pretty good motive for me.'

Wolfe folded his arms, triumphantly across his vast chest.

The man was wrong.

I shook my head slowly, 'I don't think so,' I replied. 'Yes, John and Sylvia Simmons certainly had a motive for wanting to see Lord Dunning dead, but more than that, they wanted to see him ruined, exposed for what he had done. I don't think they're into the Old Testament stuff of *an eye for an eye*. Besides, why kill Carpenter and Mark, they had no part in their daughter's death?'

Wolfe nodded slowly, digesting every word carefully. 'So,' he mumbled after a few seconds of deep concentration, 'you think it was Stanford and Drake?'

Trevalian's jaw dropped open. 'My God! Next you'll be saying it was Jayne Frobisher and Lady Barton.' He threw his hands up in complete despair at Wolfe's groundless accusations.

'No, although I think, from what I found in their rooms, John Simmons was paying someone to dig the dirt on Dunning and I believe that that person is, or was Brian Drake,' I announced, trying to defuse the obvious tension which existed now between the two men.

Wolfe stared at Trevalian, his eyes narrowing in suspicion and anger. Trevalian was staring at Wolfe coldly, it was apparent that Trevalian had no time for wild speculation which is exactly what Wolfe was doing, deliberately or otherwise, I couldn't tell.

'So, it was Drake then,' mumbled Donald slowly from his position near the door.

'Again, no. Drake was blackmailing Dunning, something about the *Yorkshire Project*, whatever that is.'

This was more than Trevalian could obviously stand. 'Cole, what the hell is it you're trying to say!' He almost snapped the words at me. He snatched another wooden chair from beneath a nearby reading table and dropped his athletic frame heavily on to it. 'For God's sake explain will you!'

'Well, put simply, I can think of a motive for almost everyone here this weekend.'

'Yes, I understand that,' agreed Trevalian, nodding quickly in agreement. 'Lord Dunning did seem to be a little pissed at having us all here, I got the feeling there was no love lost.'

'Oh yeah, you could certainly feel the love in that room,' mumbled Wolfe, more to himself than anyone directly.

'But I have no axe to grind with Lord Dunning, nor Carpenter and I don't even know Mark, I never spoke to him during the sea crossing, he seemed a little preoccupied.' Trevalian sounded quite affronted at the merest suggestion that he could ever harbour ill thoughts against anyone.

'Yes, but you did know all about that currie poison,' said Wolfe, his words coming slowly, weighted down with accusation, his eyes and tone adopting a suspicious inference, his head lolling slightly to the left, questioningly, an eyebrow raised, his eyes narrowed and fixed inquisitively on the doctors seated body.

'Well yes. I know but… And it's curare, not currie. Big difference, huge in fact.'

'True,' I mumbled, 'one can take your breath away, the other can take your breath away for a hell of a lot longer.'

'Look! I had nothing to do with any of the deaths. You must believe me.' Trevalian was almost pleading with us. Any more forceful and he would have been on his knees, hands clasped in prayer.

'Gentlemen, I do have an idea as to exactly who is responsible for these deaths. But I need to try and draw them out. I need your help.'

'What do you want us to do?' asked Donald, voting himself in as spokesman for the group.

'All I need you to do, is to keep an eye on the other guests. I don't know what reaction to expect from the others, it is possible that I may have missed some alliances.'

'What do you expect to happen?' asked Wolfe, edging forward on his seat.

'If I'm right, it is possible that the reaction could be fairly violent and dangerous, just follow my lead.'

'Count me in,' nodded Trevalian, standing, 'ready when you are.'

'As long as I get an exclusive on all this,' agreed Wolfe, smiling and forcing himself off the wooden chair. Casually, he massaged blood back into his legs.

'Don't let Mary get hurt,' was all Donald said as he moved to open the study door.

'The cavalry should be on their way,' I said, checking my watch. 'It's show time, be careful.'

Together, unified, we left the study.

Donald said it all, 'And now, to unmask a killer,' as he closed the door behind us.

I reached the drawing room and met Donald waiting nervously outside.

'Everyone here?' I asked, almost as nervous as the wreck of a man standing in front of me.

He nodded. 'Yes, they keep asking why, though.'

'Not to worry, all will be revealed,' I replied. Taking a deep breath, in what I hoped was going to be a smooth entrance, I pushed open the door and strode in, *attitude and purpose* as my old tutor used to say, won over the audience, no matter how hostile.

I hoped he was right.

The drawing room was dominated by a huge, larger than life, or death picture of the late Lord Dunning, if that was at all possible. It dwarfed the smaller and more tasteful family portrait of the smiling Dunning family in forgotten, happier times. Lord and Lady Dunning with their beautiful daughter. I got the impression, looking at my beloved Judy in the painting, it was very old, the happier times long since gone. The single massive painting of the deceased lord loomed high overhead, centrally placed above the unlit, empty stone fireplace. From here, even in death, he could still scoff at those he felt were beneath him.

Again, the usual highly polished oak panelling lined the walls, huge leaded windows overlooked the sweeping, chipped driveway at the front of the house.

I glanced quickly outside, the sun shining high above us, the storm clouds and strong winds of the previous days had vanished.

The room was now occupied by the invited dinner guests, Lady Dunning and Judy, John and Sylvia Simmons, Henry Stanford, Brian Drake, Jayne Frobisher, Major and Lady Forsythe and Lady Barton all stood waiting anxiously, fidgeting and making nervous small talk. Standing unobtrusively at the back of the room was Mary.

As Trevalian, Wolfe and Donald followed me into the room, Donald pulled the door closed behind us and then, with arms folded across his chest, he positioned himself behind me. Strategically between the party guests and the door back into the hallway, there were no other exits.

Mary crossed the room, head down and, obviously upset, she took her place beside her husband.

'Please, be seated,' I said, indicating everyone to occupy one of the many large leather seats that occupied this room.

'Cole, why have you asked us all to meet here?' It was Judy, the rough edge to her normally soft voice speaking volumes making it obvious that she had been crying. I knew that this was the last thing she needed, but I also knew that I had to go through with it.

'I believe your father's murderer to be here, in this room, with us right now,' I stated calmly.

More for effect than necessity, I began to pace around the room, I tried to keep my eyes from falling on any one person for more than a few seconds. I had time to fill, a murderer's hand to force.

I wondered if the murderer was going to take the bait and play their hand, or would they simply let me complete my announcement? Would sheer bravado and their ego get the better of them, did they think they had outsmarted me?

All questions that I knew would be answered within the next few minutes. I just hoped my plan worked.

Now they were playing my game, by my rules, and I was adamant that I was going to win.

'Thank you, ladies and gentlemen, if you would like to make yourselves comfortable, I will talk you through the events of the last few days as I see them.' I put on my best lecturing voice and hoped that I could carry this off.

'It is a textbook fact that for almost every murder, we need to have a motive. Motiveless murders are few and far between, although of course we have all heard of the psychopathic killer who needlessly kills complete strangers. However, it must be said, I believe that no one here falls into that category or comes close to fulfilling that particular profile. And motive we certainly have.'

Lady Dunning gasped.

'Hah!' sneered the major. 'Motive, motive, motive. For God's sake man, why does there have to be a motive, couldn't it be that someone here, anyone of us had had enough of the old bastard and did away with him.' It was more an accusation than a question and I acknowledged the challenge immediately.

'There was a motive major, that much is obvious.'

'How?' challenging me again.

'Simple, we can determine that by the meticulous planning which has gone into this murder, of course there have been unexpected obstacles and targets of opportunity, but they have been removed just as forcibly as the intended victim.'

'What planning?' Judy quietly asked, I'm sure she didn't really want to hear an answer, but she got one anyway.

'Your father, had to be in the study for the assassin to strike. No one could predict when in fact that would happen, nor whether or not the curtains would be open, the lights on, what the weather was going to be doing, too many variables. Besides, the burglary last week upholds the theory of a planned killing and, finally; even psychotics have never yet been documented as just deciding, on the spur of the moment to island hop across stormy seas, land on an unused jetty, pop up to a house on the hill, and kill off the lord who lives there. But please, as I said, let me continue, all will become clear soon, trust me.'

It was more than a hope, it was a desperate prayer that my idea would work.

Trevalian and Wolfe made their way to comfortable, high backed chairs positioned well back against the wall to the right of the door through which we had entered. From there, they watched the bemused faces of the partygoers with obvious interest, I watched them for several seconds, no signal, yet.

'Lady Barton,' I said, turning my attention to the white haired old woman, still immaculately dressed, sitting on the settee in the centre of the room. 'Could you remind me please, how long have you known Lord Dunning?'

'Oh... For many years, more than I care to remember, but I have had very little to do with the family since Lord Dunning was removed from the House of Lords.'

'And since that time, you have had no contact with any member of the household?' I asked, sneaking a look at my watch covertly.

'Well of course, I have been in touch from time to time, though I must admit that more recently I have been writing to Lady Dunning, in reply to her many letters of correspondence to me, she is always telling me of her marital problems and...'

'I wrote to you in the strictest of confidences!' shouted Lady Dunning. She started to sob into her hands once more, 'You have no right telling everyone about my personal problems. Martin is dead, what went on in my own home is my business and no one else's.' The sobbing increased.

'Oh, I am so sorry my dear, I thought that it might be important or relevant to Mr Meredith. After all, he only wants the truth.' Lady Barton winked at me, a twinkle in her eye.

I found it difficult to figure out if Lady Barton was genuinely concerned or sarcastic to her ladyship's plight.

I decided on the latter.

Lady Barton was obviously a lot smarter and quicker on the uptake than most people perceived, probably to their cost. I mentally labelled her a cunning old trout, someone not to underestimate or get on the wrong side of.

I turned quickly to face Judy's mother.

'Lady Dunning!' My sudden, movement, with the brusque address, caused the recent widow to spring away from me slightly, a defensive move or a natural reaction, to evade perceived violence, I did not know, but the sobbing instantly ceased.

'You were the last person amongst us here to see your husband, Lord Dunning alive, is that correct?'

'Cole, my mother knows who her husband was.' The cold, barbed, pointed comment was fired from Judy's mouth. I sensed a rapid closing of the Dunning family ranks.

'Of course she does,' I apologised, 'perhaps I should rephrase the question?' Before anyone could reply I hastily continued, 'Lady Dunning, you were the last person to see your husband alive, is that correct?'

'Yes.' The answer came in one word, long and drawn out, it seemed to last for several seconds, the tone questioning, the expression on her face curious, the rapid movement of her eyes revealed that she was thinking hastily, probably wondering where the next question would lead and what verbal traps I might be setting for her in which to snare herself.

'Apart from the killer of course,' she added.

I knew this was a cop out, a throw away comment, a desperate escape bid. In preparation for an alibi, I sensed she was already preparing if the right question was asked.

'Of course,' I replied. I knew I was being patronising, condescending in my own way, a fault Judy had nagged me about constantly.

'And I have no motive,' she continued haughtily.

'Really?'

'Yes Cole, really. I loved my husband in my own way.'

'No motive? How about this then,' I replied. 'How about a way out of a marriage you no longer wished to be a part of?' I looked straight at the woman's face, hands clasped tightly behind my back in my best most practised lecturers pose. After several seconds, and a rapid trawl through her planned escape routes, she opted for:

'I could have got a divorce,' she looked to Judy who was looking at me, 'had I wanted one.' she brushed a stray hair from her face, her eyes staring at me coldly.

'Yes, that is absolutely correct, you could have got a divorce, couldn't you. Using infidelity with Miss Frobisher as an excuse perhaps, but what would you have done about the scandal?'

Jayne Frobisher visibly squirmed under the instant gaze suddenly thrust upon her. She shifted uneasily, her eyes dipping to the carpeted floor and staying there.

'Cole!' shouted Judy sharply. 'What are you trying to imply? What are you trying to say about my mother!' She stood up, hands on hips and head cocked to one side, her verbal fighting stance adopted once again.

In the past I had always backed down, but I knew that on this occasion, neither retreat nor submission was an option open to me.

'Judy, sit down please and listen. This is what you wanted, this is what you asked for, remember?'

Slowly, confused, she sagged back on to the couch next to her mother.

'Now Lady Dunning, who would have handled your divorce? The family solicitors? Holliday, Carpenter and Drax?'

'Yes, of course.'

'Which partner? Mr Carpenter?'

'No...'

'No,' I interrupted, 'you never got on with him did you, he was more concerned with looking after your husband's interests, like his new will.'

'Yes, but...'

'The will you do not yet know the contents of. The will you tried to get access to through Mr Carpenter and, when he refused to give you the access you wanted, you went to the senior partner, Mr Holliday.'

'How do you...' Lady Dunning leapt to her feet.

'He told you that while Mr Carpenter was in charge of the case, he had no power to help you.'

I glanced quickly at my watch, it had been nearly forty minutes since I threw the table down the stairs in the hidden arms locker, time was running out on me fast.

'Let me explain what happened on the night your husband was killed.'

Slowly Lady Dunning sat back down. Judy offered her a hand to hold which her mother gratefully accepted.

'Stephen Carpenter, was in pain from his wisdom tooth operation earlier in the day. He retired early to bed. In an act of kindness and compassion, you gave Donald a decanter of whisky to take upstairs, to give to Carpenter to help numb the pain and help him sleep.'

She nodded. 'Yes, so? There is no crime in helping the sick.'

'This was the same whisky that you had given to your husband a few days prior, to celebrate his winning the paternity case. Lord Dunning told you that the whisky was off, it tasted bitter.'

'Yes, that's right and we returned the batch.'

'All bar one bottle. The opened one, the bitter one which you took charge of personally to dispose of. The whisky that was laced with curare, a vegetable-based, very lethal poison, native to Central and Northern South America. The poison, however, is only lethal if injected. Curare is harmless if swallowed, it leaves only a bitter taste.'

'But…'

'Lord Dunning drank the poisoned whisky, he noted its bitter taste and told Donald to dispose of it. When it failed to kill him on this occasion, you decided to keep it, just in case another opportunity showed itself.

'You saw an opportunity too good to miss when you saw Stephen Carpenter. He had refused you access to the will. If something happened to him, Holliday would give you all the access you wanted, so you sent the poisoned whisky up with Donald. Stephen locked his bedroom door and then drank the laced whisky, because of the open wounds in his gums, the poison entered his bloodstream, as if the poison had been injected, as a result he died instantly.'

'This is ridiculous.'

I turned my attention back to the rest of the room.

'At 8.20 last night, Lord and Lady Dunning left the dining room which was occupied by us, the dinner guests invited by Lady Dunning; every one of the guests, except of course Judy, his daughter, had a loathing or at the very least a healthy dislike for the unwitting true host. Together Lord and Lady Dunning entered the study. At 8.30 we all heard the gunshot which we thought killed Lord Dunning.'

Everyone nodded in agreement at the facts given so far.

'I can now say with certainty, that Lord Dunning was killed by a single bullet wound to the chest.'

'Yes we all know that,' sighed the major, shaking his head slowly. 'I thought you were actually going somewhere with this charade.'

'Yes, thank you major, if I may continue.' The major put his hands in the air in a dismissive manner and I carried on.

'Thank you. As I was saying, Lord Dunning was killed by a bullet wound to the chest. This bullet was fired from a small calibre pistol at close range. The tattooing of powder casing fragments and flame marks from the combusting gases around the entry wound, confirm that the fatal round was discharged within about eight inches of the victim.'

'My dear young man,' interrupted the major once more, 'it was obviously a rifle bullet to cause that much damage, and Lady Dunning has already told you that on the night of the murder, she saw a man with a rifle standing on the balcony just outside the study window.'

I smiled a crocodile smile at the major, wide and menacing, he instantly went quiet.

'As I said,' I continued, 'Lord Dunning was killed by a single small calibre pistol, the fatal shot entering through the front of his chest, piercing his heart and exiting through his upper back. Death would have been instantaneous, or as near as dammit makes no odds.

'He collapsed back into his seat, he was already dead. At 8.30, masked by the chiming of the church clock tower bells, which chime at half past and on the hour, the M-21 rifle, stolen earlier in the week from Lord Dunning's own armoury, discharged a single round.

'The weapon was aimed, targeted if you will, on the back of the seat usually occupied by Lord Dunning, during his working day, here on the island.

'To all intents and purposes, we the intended witnesses rushed into the room and would have to say that Lord Dunning was killed by the single rifle shot.

'However, I now know this to be incorrect. The black marks on Lord Dunning's jacket, are powder burns; the tattooing around the wound and the bullet hole in the lintel above the French windows prove otherwise. They confirm that they could only have been caused by a shot discharged at close range from a low angle within the study.

'Lord Dunning was obviously not happy at having us all here.

That much is certain.

'That was Lady Dunning's plan all along, the invitations which were sent out to everyone here were all from her. Lord Dunning even told us at dinner that he objected to us being in his house, abusing his hospitality. Lady Dunning admitted then that it was she who had invited us.

'But no reason was given, we all assumed, for whatever our own reasons for wanting to be here, that it was to make peace and move on.

'The plan was simple. To populate a party with people who would do pretty much anything to see Lord Dunning dead or at least take a fall. This would of course throw suspicion off herself and her lover.'

The atmosphere in the room, already tense, tightened further, everyone felt the tension increase, tenfold, the fingers of truth starting to grip the guilty, ensnaring them with their own lies and half-truths.

The invited guests looked at each other suspiciously, apprehensive about what the next revelation would be.

'Yes, your lover, Lady Dunning. You have been having this secret relationship for several months now haven't you?'

Ashamed, broken and revealed, Lady Dunning averted her eyes from my accusing gaze. Her lips clamped shut, biting down hard to avoid any more lies escaping her mouth and burying herself further in prevarication.

'What I have said is true, isn't it major?'

'What!' the cry coming simultaneously from both Lady and Major Forsythe. I felt his exclamation and protestation lacked conviction.

'Your recent return from Belize, a Central American base for the British Army, the same location from where curare is very popular and readily available; is just too much of a coincidence. You brought some of the poison back with you and gave it to Lady Dunning to use.'

'What the bloody hell are you trying to do to me Meredith!' the major was yelling, already red in the face, he was now nearing the darker shades of purple. He jumped to his feet and waved his arms around frantically.

'I'm not trying to do anything major, except get to the truth.'

'You wouldn't know the truth if it bit you on the arse. You're nothing more than a glorified schoolteacher, what the hell do you know about any of this? This is the real world, not some bloody classroom exercise!'

'I know that major, and I say again, you are the thief, the burglar who broke into this house last Wednesday.'

'Don't be preposterous Meredith, this is slander, I'll sue your arse for every penny you'll ever earn. None of this can be proven.

I continued, unchecked, 'You knew the house would be empty, the alarm off as you had arranged with Lady Dunning.'

'For God's sake Meredith, this is my life man!'

'Again,' I continued, 'with her help, you knew the exact location of the armoury and the security measures in place, you knew the security code and entered the locker.'

'You can't prove any of that,' he stated smugly. 'It's just circumstantial, you can't back any of this up.'

The major was looking across nervously now between the accusing rage-filled eyes of Lady Forsythe and the guilt-wracked quaking body that was Lady Dunning.

'You took two weapons from the arms locker, an M-21 snipers rifle and the pistol, along with a silencer.

'You took the rifle to the church where you hid it in the church clock tower, along with a highly advanced military security camera, this you had planned to use as a decoy, had you been caught or challenged, as to why you were on the island.

'Lady Dunning had obviously told you that the church was untended during the day, which is why you oiled the hinges on the tower room door for when you came back later, just in case anyone was tending the church in the evening, you did not want to be heard.

'You knew that no one went into the church clock mechanism room at this time of year so it was safe for you to set the rifle in position; ready for your deadly deed to be done.

'You then left the church and made your way back down to the old jetty where your boat was waiting. But accidents do happen, you stepped on a rotten board on the jetty, the plank shattering and catching your foot. I suspect that that is the reason for your current leg injury, which is causing you to limp.

'In pulling your foot free, you dislodged one of your shoes, a Gucci I believe. I recovered it from the sludge and timbers beneath the jetty yesterday.'

'Excuse me, but how can that be?' asked Lady Forsythe, puzzled. 'My husband's shoes are all accounted for, they're hanging in his wardrobe even as we speak. I know because I packed them myself, I always do.'

Lady Forsythe, jumping to her husband's defence, was exactly what I had come to expect from the woman. I had only known her for a relatively short time, but I had surmised that she was loyal, faithful and trusting, to a fault, something the major had taken advantage of.

Major Forsythe did not deserve or warrant such loyalty.

'Yes, I know. And I must confess, it threw me for a while. I was fairly sure from the start that your husband was involved in this somehow, but the missing shoe would have made the case easier to prove.

'As it is, the shoes which are hanging in the wardrobe marked for Wednesday; which as we all know now was the date of the burglary, are new, they have never even been worn. These shoes are so new, that Major Forsythe has not as yet removed the tissue paper pushed into the toes of the shoes to keep their shape. If you check the soles of those shoes, you will find that they are not marked, showing that they have never been worn, whereas all the other shoes are slightly scuffed, worn or marked in some way.

'In addition to this, on the heel of these brand new shoes, there is a small round sticky area, where the price label was previously located, the other shoes do not have this mark. I suspect that the major purchases all his shoes from the same reputable, high priced store, the shoes he bought as a replacement pair, were bought, as a point of necessity, probably from a more local shoe shop, thereby being marked differently.'

'You really haven't got a clue have you,' sighed the major, shaking his head wearily again. A forced short laugh escaped his lips, I continued, much to his annoyance.

'It was you who sold the M-21 rifle to Lord Dunning, through your contact with his wife. The weapon was already sighted for yourself, Lord Dunning told me that he had never been able to adjust the sights, that was because you had permanently fixed them in place, unable to be used or changed by anyone other than yourself, the weapon was sighted for your use and you alone.

'You only had to do minor adjustments on the night, due to the inclement weather, you knew the range to the target, something you had checked and measured on your previous visit, you knew that the wind and rain could adjust the trajectory of the bullet, something which only a person familiar with firearms would be aware of.

'You were able to calculate the exact drift and drop of the round so that the bullet would drop straight through the back of the chair on which Lord Dunning was sitting; already dead, even so, congratulations, it was a hell of a shot.'

'But I was with you when the shot was fired,' he stated defensively.

'Yes, that is true, we all saw you then, but if you recall, you disappeared a short time prior to the shooting. At this time, you made your way back to the clock tower and connected the trigger mechanism of the rifle to the timing gear of the clock by the chime regulator.

'To the lay person, they would never know from just looking, which wheel did what to what, but you already have expert knowledge of clock mechanisms, from your time apprenticed to Lady Barton's husband when he ran the watch and clock repairers.'

Major Forsythe sat down stunned, reeling under the impetus of the information and deductions he had just been hit with. I checked my watch again, not long to go, I thought.

The major was looking at me with quite unrestrained hatred. There was a disconcerting vein in the right side of his neck that was pulsating violently, and the man's face had now turned completely to a dark rage.

'I understand you are expecting a motor launch to pick you up this morning,' I asked, directing the question straight at him.

He nodded slowly.

'Arranged through your assistant back on the mainland, to collect you and take you straight to your new posting in Northern

Island.'

Again he nodded slowly.

'Where is it that the launch is collecting you from?'

'The harbour of course,' he growled, his eyes narrowing, his teeth clenching hard.

'And what time is it that you arranged to be collected?'

He swallowed hard, his eyes now glancing left and right, his head barely moving. The muscles in his neck visibly tensed, and I sensed he was ready for fight or flight.

He shrugged, 'It may be delayed for a while,' he stated.

'Yes, I thought perhaps it might be.' I looked quickly at my watch and across to Donald, he was now edging slowly towards the major.

Gently he shepherded Mary to one side, Wolfe was already on his feet, moving to her side to prevent anything going wrong.

'How were these travel arrangements made? Lady Forsythe was obviously unaware of your plans when you arrived here, so they must have been made whilst you were here on the island. Is that correct major?'

He nodded once more.

'So how did you make these new career arrangements?'

'By phone,' he snapped in reply, 'how else!'

'How else indeed,' I recapped. 'You see the problem with that is the simple fact that the telephones across the whole of this island have not been working since your previous visit on Wednesday, so when you told us last night that you had just spoken to your batman on the mainland, you were lying weren't you?'

'No,' he sighed. 'Ever heard of mobile phones, this is the twenty-first century you know, people other than students do have them you know, even people like me.' He laughed at his own joke, and at my expense.

I smiled and waited for his forced laughter to subside.

'People like you and me, yes. People like Lord Dunning, no. In fact no one who lives here on the island actually has a mobile phone. They simply do not work here, the geological make-up of the rocks here prevent their working, that was one of the reasons why Dunning came here.'

Lady Dunning nodded, barely imperceptibly.

'I suspect major, that you used your time to a more deadly pursuit whilst we believed you were making the call back to the mainland.'

Donald had circled the group of dazed guests, his position now almost directly opposite mine, behind the group. As a butler, he was trained to fade into the background, to be forgotten about, which is what I was now hoping would happen.

I spoke again, intent on drawing the group's collective attention to me.

'I believe sir, that what actually happened was this. When you arrived, you went straight upstairs to your appointed bedroom, appointed by Lady Dunning at the rear of the house, well away from casual observers and with a clear run across the lawns to the church tower.

'When you got into the room, you opened the bedroom window slightly for later use.

'Later, under the pretence of chasing shadows in the dark which were, it has to be said, only seen by Lady Dunning and yourself, you went to the church, where, to your surprise, you met Mark. You made your excuses to him and went up into the clock tower, the door hinges already oiled on your previous visit, made sure that Mark did not hear you go into the clock mechanism room.

'You sighted the sniper rifle on the back of the chair in Lord Dunning's study, making the necessary adjustments for wind and rain; you knew the curtains would be open and that Lord Dunning would already be in the chair. You connected the trigger of the rifle to the timing gear in the clock tower, removed the safety catch and then returned to the house. You placed the gardener's ladder against the windowsill of your bedroom and then came back into the dining room to tell us all about the mysterious figure you had chased through the garden.

'Shortly before eight thirty, Lady Dunning took her husband into the study, where I believe she asked him for a divorce one last time. Again, he refused, as perhaps you both knew he would, after all, stubbornness was one of his many charming character flaws. I imagine that as expected, he did refuse, probably threatening that he would ensure that the major's military career would be ruined and, to add further insult to injury, Lord Dunning probably announced that he would also be telling Lady Forsythe about the affair, after all, the title is hers, the family money is hers. Of course this would result in his finances being frozen and with you both cut off from financial support, neither of you would be kept in the manner to which you have become accustomed.

'Lady Dunning then produced the pistol, previously stolen from the armoury. She manoeuvred Lord Dunning behind his desk, got him to unlock the desk drawer and then shot him through the heart. The bullet from that short a range, passed straight through his body and then exited the room through the door lintel of the French doors.

'Hardly surprising, Lord Dunning, already dead, collapsed back into his chair. Lady Dunning then opened the drawer, hiding the pistol in the drawer beneath the "Yorkshire Project" file. She locked the drawer and put the desk drawer key back into the breast pocket of her now dead husband.

'With time marching on, all she had to do was wait.'

I surveyed the room again, a strange, surreal hush had fallen over the assembled group; Judy, I noticed, was now avoiding my gaze. The major was smiling at me, slowly sipping from his recently refilled tumbler, calm, content, amused.

Lady Forsythe was wringing her hands nervously, her eyes not straying from their piercing survey of the carpet before her.

'As the church clock struck 8.30, the chime regulator gearing moved, pulled the trigger on the rifle and discharged the single round which we all initially believed was the fatal shot. Already trained on the stationary chair in which Lord Dunning was already sitting, already dead, the round shattered the back of the seat and Lord Dunning.'

'But,' challenged Lady Barton, 'Helen already told us that a man on the balcony had fired the shot through the French windows, why do you disbelieve her; couldn't she be right about that and you be mistaken? After all, she was there, you're just guessing at what might have been.'

I nodded, it was a fair challenge, but I was prepared for it.

'Unfortunately, physics will bear me out. You see the trajectory of the bullet which passed through the chair, Lord Dunning's body, his desk and finally bedded itself in the floor of the study, revealed that for it to have happened the way Lady Dunning has stated, the assailant, from where she said he was standing, would have to have been about nine feet tall at a guess. Lady Dunning also said that the man who had just shot her husband had jumped over the balcony, a drop of about ten feet, on to the croquet lawn, which, because of the rain, was soft and muddy and would easily have taken and retained the impact of such a landing, however, there was no such impression left near the balcony to support this claim.'

'Oh.' Lady Barton shrugged dismissively and glanced sideways across at Lady Dunning, her gaze did not falter.

'You will recall,' I continued, 'that Major Forsythe returned to the house wet and bedraggled, stating that he had been chasing a man in the grounds, he subsequently went upstairs, to shower and change.

'I suggest he actually did neither, straight away. Instead he went to his room, climbed out of his already open window on to the ladder he had set there previously. He climbed down the ladder and made his way across the croquet lawn back into the church. As no one was about, he disconnected the rifle from the gears but, for ease and speed, he just cut the wire that was connecting the trigger mechanism to the timing gear.

'In his haste to leave the scene, the major dropped a piece of the metal wire, which I later discovered.

'He then placed the security camera in position, secreted there in the tower on Wednesday. I found the wire underneath the camera housing, showing that the wire was there before the camera.

'The major then hid the rifle in the church intending to collect it later. He returned to the house, up the ladder, into his bathroom, change of clothes and back down to us.'

The major looked on impassively, slowly swigging from his tumbler, no trace of emotion on his face.

A universal mask of confusion was fixed immobile on the faces of the other occupants of the room. Only Judy and her mother showed any emotion. Judy was watching me disbelievingly, Lady Dunning's gaze was still fixed firmly on the carpet before her, at any moment I expected it to spontaneously burst into flames, so intense was her glare.

I tried to attract Judy's attention and to reassure her that everything was going to be fine, she saw the look in my eyes and turned her face away.

I carried on, 'Later the same evening, I went to the church, where I received this.' I indicated my injuries and drew attention to my swollen and bruised face. 'The person who gave me this, I found dead this morning.' I glanced around the silent gathering, again my gaze settling on Major Forsythe. 'I believe this is yours.' I produced the distorted golden circlet that I had taken from Mark's dead hand, his dried blood still encrusted on its broken features.

'What is it?' asked Lady Forsythe, edging closer to view the proffered item, her voice scarcely more than a whisper.

'It was a monocle,' I replied. 'I took it out of the dead boy's hands this morning. I also found a discharged cartridge, again Mark had it in his hand. He was trying to tell us who had shot him.'

'That's ridiculous,' blurted the major, slamming the tumbler down on the table with such force I expected either it or the tumbler to shatter. 'Can't you see! Can't any of you see, I have my monocle here, now. Everyone saw me with my monocle after the incident, it cannot possibly be mine.'

'Major, when I first met you, I noted that the monocle you were wearing was golden, now it is silver. Where is your gold coloured one? The one you wore when you arrived?'

'I...' He was about to deny any knowledge of the existence of the golden monocle, that much was evident from the look on his face as it contorted in the effort of lying; the look shot at him by Lady Forsythe silenced him instantly.

'Don't know,' he sighed.

'What kind of weapon was he shot by?' asked Stanford quietly.

'Probably the same weapon Lord Dunning was shot with, a pistol, probably an automatic with a noise suppresser.'

'Which you say is still locked in my father's desk drawer in the study!' challenged Judy, for the first time since I had begun to concentrate on her mother and the major's involvement in her father's death, she looked me straight in the eye.

I shook my head, 'No, the pistol is no longer in the drawer, I checked earlier this morning after I found Mark in the church, but there are signs, evidence that it was there until very recently, the oil and powder residue on the paperwork in the drawer is still fresh.'

'So where is it now?' asked Donald from the back of the room, already he was starting to move towards the main body of the group. Several of the seated persons jumped, the forgotten butler so successful in his task of hiding in plain sight.

'I think Major Forsythe can answer that one for us, can't you major?'

In one deft movement, the major, smiling dementedly, was moving away from the group, his hand snaking up from his jacket pocket, with it, clenched tightly in his right hand I saw the jet-black body of a small pistol, an automatic, the suppresser was now missing, he had no need for quiet now. The handgun was pointed menacingly towards me. Staring down the barrel, it looked several times bigger than it actually was. Everything else seemed to vanish into the background as my entire attention was focused on the barrelled death before me.

'I was right,' I called across to Donald, trying to front out the confrontation, 'a 9mm automatic.'

'Yes, Mr Meredith, you did very well, right on all counts it would seem. Shame it's all in vain though isn't it,' he sneered.

'Major, you can't possibly believe that you can get away with this, everyone here is a witness. They all know what you've both done. You can't escape, the police will find you wherever you go, you do know that.'

'Alan,' Lady Dunning's voice croaked from the couch to my right. 'Did you... Did you have to kill Mark?' Perhaps the shreds of her conscience were now beginning to show through, an eleventh hour twinge of guilt perhaps.

'Yes darling, I had to.'

Such passion in his voice, behind the mask of the executioner. A once noble and loving man still lived, if I could reach him, negotiate with him, I knew that the incident could end here and now, without further bloodshed.

'Oh, well if you had to, you had to.' She accepted his reply without question.

My views on Judy's mother were going downhill rapidly and gaining speed.

Time seemed to slow, I sensed rather than saw Donald leap towards the gunman, Forsythe turned and I heard the awful bark of the pistol, the spent cartridge cartwheeling, spinning, flying off into the furthest corner of the room.

Donald seemed to change direction mid leap, his heavy athletic frame crashing to the floor in a crumpled mess, the table on which his flailing arm collided disintegrating under the sudden impact.

Wolfe grabbed Mary's arm, as screaming, she tried to reach her fallen husband.

Michael Trevalian was also on his feet, making a beeline straight for Donald, again, the awful roar of the pistol stopped him dead in his tracks. I saw the surprise on his face as he looked down and witnessed the deep crimson patch spreading from his shattered right shoulder. Trevalian's eyes slid shut and he too was slammed to the floor.

Screams erupted around me, confusion reigned. Above the clamour of the frightened men and women, I heard Forsythe yelling for quiet.

The pistol snapped twice more, shattering the beautiful ceiling rose and sending dust and plaster crashing to the floor around us.

Silence came reluctantly, Donald was moving slowly, painfully on the floor, groaning in agony. Trevalian remained still, his body hardly moving, barely perceptible, though he was still breathing. The slow rise and fall of his chest told me that for the time being, at least, he was alive.

'Shit! I think he's dead!' Wolfe whispered harshly from my right.

Again Forsythe trained the pistol on me and with a flick of his wrist motioned for me to join the others.

Lady Dunning, crossed the room to be at his side.

'Just how far do you think you'll get, Forsythe?' I asked, attempting to adopt Judy's cocked head, hands on hip stance. It needed work.

'The police will be here soon.'

He laughed, loud and long. 'You're not the only one with a good memory, Meredith, I know that the police cannot possibly be coming can they, you told us yesterday you had phoned them, and a few minutes ago you told us that the phones don't work do they.'

'He's right you know,' acknowledged Lady Barton, nodding.

I smiled, my time was definitely running out, I was heavily into borrowed time.

'You know what, Meredith, you're right about the witnesses, you've dug the graves for all of them.'

He was giggling as he used the pistol to indicate the group, 'No one will find you here for days, we'll be miles away by then, with new identities and monies already transferred.'

Outside and overhead, I was suddenly aware of the heavy rhythmic beating of a rotary powered aircraft, its engines getting louder and louder as it neared.

'Who? What is that?' asked Forsythe, the grin disappearing from his face as the engine noise droned ever louder and ever nearer.

'It's the police,' I sighed, 'I told you they were coming.'

It was my turn to smile as I looked back at my watch, forty-eight minutes I noted, they must have been on a coffee break.

'NO!'

I heard Forsythe scream and then several more loud roars ripped through the air, a decanter near my right arm disintegrated under the sudden, unseen impact, the door jamb behind me splintered and shattered and the carpeted floor raced up to meet me, as I dived behind the relative protection of the couch for safety.

The windows to the front of the house suddenly exploded outwards and from my prone position on the floor, I saw a heavy antique-looking wooden stool leaving via the shattered windows followed almost immediately by the major.

I jumped to my feet, performed a quick inventory of body functions, everything was where I needed it, thankfully there were no extra holes for me to worry about.

'Wolfe,' I yelled, whilst starting to turn towards the destroyed window, 'stay here, get someone to look after Donald and Michael, I'm going after the major.'

Without waiting for the reply, I was leaping through the ruined window and racing across the shale and stone driveway after the fleeing shape of the major.

Despite his leg injury, he was already turning the few scant seconds head start he had into a widening gap and I subconsciously found myself marvelling and cursing at the fitness of the British army.

Behind me, and over towards the croquet lawn, behind the house, the pitch of the helicopter's engines had changed and I knew that it was landing, but I could not concern myself with that as the major was gaining ground, widening the gap with every stride.

He suddenly turned and vanished through the tree-lined avenue. It only took a few seconds for me to reach the narrow gap in the trees through which the major had disappeared.

My lungs were screaming in submission and my muscles ached as I pounded heavily off the driveway and through the small gap in the trees which lined the picturesque avenue. Trees with which I had been so impressed on my arrival were now no more than a scenic hindrance, offering the protection of cover to both myself and my nemesis.

The major had come this way, I knew that for certain, but to exactly where he had gone, once out of my sight, I was less sure.

Caution screamed a loud warning in the back of my head and thoughts of the encounter in the church the previous evening promptly ached as if on cue to remind me that pain was a very real alternative to caution.

I took full advantage of this respite, lowering myself down low at the base of what I hoped was a sturdy enough tree trunk.

I took greedy gulps of air, attempting to stop the burning pain in my lungs and the incessant loud pounding of my pumping heart, as it rung deafeningly but reassuringly in my ears.

A little off to my right, I heard the distinctive gentle rustle of undergrowth as someone or something slowly meandered through it. Slowly, I turned my head towards the sound, forcing my breath to quieten down.

I did not wish my last breath to be the one that got me killed and was now coming to realise that only in films did the foolish hero, unarmed and stupid, chase after a man with a gun through the undergrowth. A man who had already proven himself capable of killing.

About twenty feet away I could see the distinct bulk of the major, he was keeping low, his body sliding, barely above the level of the thick foliage, he was moving slowly and I realised that it was not in fact him that I heard moving at all, but a small grey rabbit several feet in front of him. Luck was obviously on my side. He did not appear to have seen me.

A friend I had met at university and with whom I had shared a room, was now gainfully employed as a master illusionist. He went by the stage name of Stephen St George, real name Steve Barclay. At university he had supplemented his meagre student loan by performing children's magic shows.

One thing I had learnt from the great St George was that it was always movement that got you caught, if you wanted someone to look at your right hand, you moved it while the left hand was performing the real magic of moving the mirrors and making smoke, or something like that.

Anyway, I knew that if I moved, the major and his new found friend would see me. From this range, I doubted as to whether the major, an experienced soldier, would miss.

I could see the major clearly, he was carefully looking around him, obviously, with more luck than judgement, I was better hidden than I had first thought.

Slowly, like some great serpent, he slithered on his belly back into the undergrowth and, almost silently, he was gone. I gave myself a few minutes to get my breath back, and then, in a crouch, I edged myself towards where I had last seen the major. The broken bracken and bent foliage clearly marked his route away from the driveway and towards the old disused harbour.

An escape route?

It took me only a few more minutes to work my way through the rough shrubbery and prickly gorse until at last I reached a narrow worn path. Instinctively I knew that it was leading towards the old jetty. I picked up my pace and trotted briskly down towards the sea front.

I reached the rough, worn steps and unevenly eroded path that led steeply down to the narrow shale beach. I suddenly heard several loud cracks rip through the salty air. Simultaneously, I was aware of a terrible tearing sensation in my left arm, tremendous pain, heat and momentum spinning me round backwards.

The first thought through my mind was *the bastard is shooting*!

The second thought, *he's shot me*!

The third thought, quickly overtaking the first two was simply, *Oh shit*!

I felt my feet go out from under me. My left arm, useless and burning, could do nothing to stop me from falling the remaining twenty feet or so on to the unyielding rocky beach.

Bright pinpricks of light exploded across my eyes as the air was smashed from me as I landed heavy and awkward on the uneven stones on the pebble and rock dashed beach. Weak, unable to force myself over on to my back, I knew that something was broken, I just hoped to hell it wasn't something important.

Darkness washed over me like a wave. I was vaguely aware that it was a shadow, deep and black, cast by someone who was now standing almost directly over me. A voice, heavy, slow and with far too much echo boomed above me, with effort, I was able to make out the voice of the major.

'And this is how it ends Meredith, you dead on the beach, me hiding out till sundown and then stealing a boat and away to a new life, alas, sadly alone, but with a new identity and enough money to keep me out of the hands of the law forever.

I tried to speak but managed only a whimper, 'Goodbye, Mr Meredith.'

I heard the body of the automatic being drawn back, the unmistakable sound of the round being chambered, the weapon cocked, ready to spell my death in loud, monosyllabic tones, when from far away, another voice, as muffled as the first boomed into life.

'Armed police, put the gun down!'

I sensed rather than saw the major raise the gun towards my head, as I lay prone and unmoving on the beach. Two rapid loud explosions from the cliff top were the last things I heard.

With a Herculean effort, I forced my eyes open.

My arms both felt uncomfortable and stiff. I risked a glance to my left, my arm was blooded and bound. Wires and tubes were protruding from it at many oblique angles. A look to my right greeted me with a similar scene, although this time my arm was sandwiched between two unyielding, unmoving boards. A white, sharp, jagged piece of shattered bone was protruding clearly from my lower forearm, a compound fracture.

The realisation forced itself through the warm, fuzzy drug induced feeling that had enshrouded my brain and the world crashed back into darkness once more.

The looming scene of the hospital encroached ever closer as we approached from the air filtering through my flickering eyelids as consciousness came and went.

I was vaguely aware of the heavy presence of a police officer in thick, unyielding body armour supporting my upper body in his arms, as I was assisted out of the makeshift air ambulance, my return to the mainland had ensued far quicker and far more painfully and disorientating than I had ever envisioned.

I was vaguely aware of two other makeshift stretchers being unslung from the sides of the helicopter as darkness once more crashed over me.

Later, once the sedatives had worn off and the full brunt of the pain resulting from my recent injuries returned, just to let me know how much I really need to listen and pay attention to the little voice inside when the word caution is screamed, I was allowed visitors.

The police first asked their questions about what had happened, what I knew, what I had seen. They told me that Lady Dunning had fully admitted her part in the deaths of both her husband and the solicitor, Stephen Carpenter. She had, reluctantly, handed over the casing of the bullet which had discharged the fatal round that killed Lord Dunning. She had, they said, collected it, still warm from the study floor, wanting to keep it as a memento, a trophy, the key to her new freedom. The Pavulon, in the whisky, she had told them, was the medical name of the curare poison Forsythe had given her. She had shown no remorse. I found myself wondering if I had mentioned the Pavulon name to Trevalian when I had first discovered it. Could lives have been saved? I did not know. Was I to blame?

My statement made, I was allowed to rest, briefly, before the next horde descended upon me: journalists, reporters, hacks, whatever you want to call them. I quickly realised that few, if any, of them were interested in the truth. Scandal sold papers, that was all they wanted. What I didn't say, I was sure they were going to quote.

Wolfe was noticeable by his absence, probably a deadline somewhere; I knew where his priorities lay.

Then it was the doctors, pushing and prodding me, bending limbs and rotating joints.

And then the most painful visit of all.

Judy arrived.

She explained that the major had been shot by a police marksman on the beach as he prepared to finish me off. Her mother, Lady Dunning had been arrested, charged with the murder of her husband and Stephen Carpenter.

Then those terrible words, I knew deep inside were coming, 'I hold you responsible for this Cole, you told everyone about my mother's part in this. I can never forgive you.'

Cold, emotionless words, spat with hate as I lay here, mummified and wired to the national grid.

'Judy, darling, I only told the truth,' I tried to explain. 'You asked me to do it, remember?' My restrained state forbidding the use of my arms, which I knew I used excessively in speech, but I wanted to hold her, to hug her and tell her everything would be all right.

But I could not.

'I think we should end this, now.'

It was a statement of closure, the timetable set in stone.

I noticed that the engagement ring I had saved so hard for all those years ago, was now missing from her left hand. Gently, with something akin to the tenderness she once held for me, she placed it carefully on the bedside table, where I could see it but where I could not reach.

'Goodbye, Cole.'

With that, she turned and was gone. Once again, I was all alone, unable to keep hold of the woman who meant everything to me.

Perhaps my old man was right all along; I was the great white hopeless.

I was out of hospital two weeks later and back at the university, I was hailed a hero by my students and the faculty. At home, in the bare flat where Judy and I had once shared so many wonderful memories and happy times; without her I just sat alone in the darkness, in silence. I felt destined to spend my life alone, ignoring the constant ringing phone and personal calls from my parents and siblings, friends and colleagues who all knew what was best for me.

I heard Donald was convalescing back on the island; Judy was keeping him on there to run things.

Michael Trevalian and his wife had opened the surgery, a few weeks late, but he too was on the mend.

Wolfe was somewhere in Columbia, doing an exposé story on drug barons and their European cartels.

I had been out of hospital a week, it was a Sunday, a day I shall never forget. The knock at the flat door came soft and rhythmically, a peculiar knock I had long since forgotten, the knock of a friend, one who had had no need to knock our door for many months.

Like a shot, I was out of the seat and reaching for the light switch. I pulled the door open in one swift movement.

A gentle, soft voice, as sweet as I remembered, greeted me.

'Cole? Hi, it's me, can we talk?'

Judy was back.

But was our relationship strong enough to last? That is a

question only time will allow us to answer. We have agreed to work at it, together.

I hope we will succeed.